American Dreams

"Did you have a good time?" Michael asked.

Is he kidding? Meg thought. "Good? No. That's not the word for it," she said slowly, wanting to capture the exact words to express her feelings. "I mean, I can't imagine anything that'll ever feel so . . . so . . . important. So exactly what I want to do all the time."

"To be on TV?" Michael asked.

"Yeah, on it," Meg agreed. She paused. It was more than that. "But even *around* it. The music, the other kids, Mr. Clark . . . the whole thing." She looked down self-consciously. "That probably sounds silly to you."

Michael shook his head. "No. Sounds a lot like me on my first day. I'm Michael Brooks, the Associate Producer of the show."

Meg extended her hand. "I'm Meg Pryor."

American Dreams

Dance with Me

Adapted by Emily Oz from the television series created by
Jonathan Prince from the teleplays written by Jonathan Prince,
Becky Hartman Edwards, Emily Whitesell, Jon Harmon
Feldman, John Romano, Rama Stagner, Becky Hartman
Edwards & John Romano, Jon Feldman, Sherri Cooper,
Deborah Swisher, Liz Tigelaar, Michael Foley, David Harris &
Christine Schenley, and John Cowan & Robert Rovner

SIMON SPOTLIGHT™

New York   London   Toronto   Sydney

This book is a work of fiction. Any references to historical events, real people, or real locales are used fictitiously. Other names, characters, places, and incidents are the product of the author's imagination, and any resemblance to actual events or locales or persons, living or dead, is entirely coincidental.

Simon Spotlight
An imprint of Simon & Schuster Children's Publishing Division
1230 Avenue of the Americas, New York, New York 10020
© 2004 NBC Studios, Inc. and Universal Network Television LLC. *American Dreams*, its characters, and related trademarks and copyrights are the property of NBC Studios, Inc. and Universal Network Television LLC. Licensed by Universal Studios Licensing LLLP.
All rights reserved, including the right of reproduction in whole or in part in any form.

SIMON SPOTLIGHT and colophon are registered trademarks of Simon & Schuster.
Manufactured in the United States of America
First Edition 10 9 8 7 6 5 4 3 2 1
ISBN 0-689-87080-9
Library of Congress Control Number: 2003114491

Dance with Me

Prologue

WFIL Studios was, without a doubt, the place to be. After all, WFIL was home to *American Bandstand*, the hot new program that had captured the entire country's attention. *Bandstand* attracted the top performers, and in addition to the regular dancers who appeared on the show, a handful of lucky teens were selected to be on national TV. It was heaven, definitely the place to be.

Or so Meg Pryor thought.

She couldn't be sure, since for weeks now, she and her best friend, Roxanne Bojarski, had been patiently waiting on line in the hopes that the line guy would notice them and give them access to the enchanted kingdom.

It didn't seem to be working. Roxanne executed a few of her best dance moves just for good measure, and Meg joined in, but the line guy wasn't biting. To be fair, just about everyone else on line was dancing, too, so it was no wonder that he hadn't picked the two of them. But . . . they came literally *every* week.

That had to count for something . . . didn't it? *Can't he see how much I need to be in there?* Meg thought, frowning. *No one on this line could possibly want this as badly as Roxanne and I do.*

The sound of high-pitched shrieking drew the girls' attention. Jimmy Riley, *Bandstand* regular, was making his way into the studio for the afternoon taping. "Jimmy Riley! Rox, Jimmy Riley!" Meg squealed, squeezing her friend's arm in excitement.

Naturally, Roxanne had already spotted him, but was doing her best to appear unfazed. "He looks taller in person," she said blithely.

"Wouldn't you die just to meet him? Forget even dancing with him," Meg gushed, breathless.

"All right, that's it for today. Thanks for coming down," the line guy said, dismissing the hopefuls.

Meg sighed and checked her watch quickly. "He ran late today. We've only got twelve minutes." There was no way they'd make it back home without missing the beginning of *Bandstand*!

Roxanne raised an eyebrow calmly. "No problem," she replied. "Shortcut?"

Meg shrugged. "No choice."

Like clockwork, the girls flew across the busy downtown Philly street, deftly avoiding oncoming cars and weaving their way among the pedestrians.

They sped around the street corner just as their bus was preparing to pull away.

Roxanne put two fingers in her mouth and whistled. The bus ground to a halt and the girls hopped on, relieved.

"Like I said, Meg, no problem," Roxanne announced confidently, grinning as the girls reached their stop and jumped off the bus. They ran down the sidewalk and past Meg's younger brother, Will, in the Pryor's front yard. "You're not gonna make it," Will proclaimed solemnly, tossing a football into the air as the girls whizzed by. His bad leg dragged in its polio brace.

"I love you too, Will," Roxanne shouted, without breaking stride.

The girls raced through the front door and into the den, where Mrs. Pryor stood ready to shut off the television now that her cooking program was over.

"Don't," Meg shrieked. "Don't turn it off!" She and Roxanne slid into position on the couch, where they could be found at 4 P.M. every afternoon. Meg forced herself to take a deep breath. Casting a sidelong glance at Roxanne, she saw that her friend shared none of her panic.

"Like I said," Roxanne quipped, "no problem."

On TV, Dick Clark was announcing today's

guest. "Outside we have a surprise November snowstorm, but in here, it's a 'Heatwave.' Please welcome Martha and the Vandellas!"

As the music cued up, Meg and Roxanne leaped out of their seats. As far as Meg was concerned, dancing to *Bandstand*—even if she had to do it in her own living room—was the best part of the afternoon! She was so glad that Roxanne felt the same way.

Just like she'd been doing every night since they were five, Roxanne stayed for dinner that evening. And just like they had every night since they were five, after dinner Meg and Roxanne went up to the bedroom that Meg shared with her younger sister, Patty, to hang out, gossip, and listen to records. Roxanne mugged in Meg's goofy band hat and continued the dance party around the bedroom, smoking a cigarette as she moved, fanning the smoke toward the open window. She relayed to Meg the details of her latest date: ". . . and I'm kissing him and guess what he smells like?"

Meg couldn't imagine. Fifteen years old, and she'd never even been on a date, much less kissed a boy. "Fish," she said, guessing wildly. "Do you think Gina Rizzelli's boobs are too big?"

"Fish? Meg, what kind of an answer is that?" Rox

asked. "Limes. That's what he smelled like. Limes."

Meg couldn't think of an especially good reason why a boy would smell of limes. Unexpected smells were just one more aspect of kissing that she wasn't sure she was prepared to deal with. The doorknob rattled, but the door didn't open. Meg had locked it, as Patty was always wanting to nose in on her conversations with Roxanne. Patty was super-smart and precocious, and could always be counted on to know what was going on with anyone in the Pryor household . . . so it was of supreme importance to exercise discretion when she was around.

"Mom says you're not allowed to lock our door," Patty called insistently from the hallway.

Roxanne coolly hid her lit cigarette behind the band hat while Meg fanned the smoke out the open window with a magazine. "It's not locked, Patty. Try again," Roxanne yelled through the door. To Meg she said, "And Gina Rizzelli's a cow." Which was, Meg had to concede, at least partly true.

"It is so locked!" Patty protested.

"If she's such a cow, why do all the boys like her so much?" Meg asked. She really wanted to know.

"Because she puts out," Roxanne said simply, as Meg grimaced and opened the door for Patty.

"What are you guys doing?" Patty demanded.

"Nothing that you can do. So get whatever you need and leave," Meg said.

"Mom said you have to try to be nicer to me," Patty replied.

"I *am* trying," Meg said.

"Well, try harder. Starting immediately," Patty insisted, as Meg pushed her out the door.

"Good-bye, Patty," Meg said, slamming the door behind her sister.

Roxanne smiled mischievously, brown eyes twinkling. She was an only child and while she was practically part of the Pryor family, she relished the idea of having siblings—even if they were annoying. "Who really gives a rip about Gina Rizzelli?" she asked, turning the conversation back to the topic at hand.

"It's just that . . . ," Meg began. "It's just that she gets everything she wants. She's a cheerleader and Frank Romano likes her and she got to model once in that catalog. I mean, don't you ever worry that you won't get the things you want?"

Meg was serious about this. Sure, she had friends at East Catholic, and she thought she was pretty enough, and her family loved her nothing was really *wrong* with her life, she knew. But nothing had *happened*, either.

That was part of the reason why she was so determined to dance on *Bandstand*. There was the fun of dancing and the excitement of seeing famous musicians perform live, and of course it would be amazing to actually appear on national television. But her need was bigger than that. She couldn't necessarily put it into words, but she felt like being on *Bandstand* would *mean* something. And she was going to make sure it happened, no matter what.

Roxanne was still considering Meg's last comment. "No," she said, demonstrating yet again how supremely self-confident she was. "I never worry about not getting what I want."

"I do," Meg insisted, her voice plaintive. "I don't want to be one of those people who never has anything special happen." She sat on the edge of her bed and looked squarely at her friend.

"You're special," Roxanne assured her.

"How?" Meg asked, genuinely curious.

Roxanne paused contemplatively. "You're really nice," she answered.

Meg's ego deflated in one big *whoosh*. "*Nice?* That's all? I mean, come on——if I died tomorrow, what would people say?"

From behind the door came a defiant, "Good

riddance!" After a moment, Patty added, "I wasn't listening!"

Frustrated, Meg threw a book at the door. It landed on the floor with a resounding *thud*, doing nothing to make her feel better.

This is really not the type of music I'd like to be hearing, Meg thought to herself as she finished band practice. She still had the song "Heatwave" stuck in her head— maybe because her geeky uniform was hot and her hat was rubbing her forehead the wrong way.

As she leaned down to pack her clarinet back into its case, Roxanne rushed up to her. "Ask me what I'm doing this Saturday," she said breathlessly.

Meg shrugged. "I don't want to play this game."

"Ask me," Roxanne insisted.

Meg took a deep breath. "What are you doing on Saturday?" she said dutifully.

"Oh, just hanging out with my good friends the Ronettes and the Beach Boys on *American Bandstand,*" Roxanne said casually.

Meg's jaw dropped open. "What? How do you know the line guy will let you in?" she demanded.

"Because he and I have an understanding," Roxanne explained.

"Since when?" Meg asked, suspicious.

"Since Tuesday night when we made out," Roxanne admitted, not the least bit ashamed.

"Roxanne!" Meg squealed, somewhat shocked.

But mostly envious.

"Fine, be that way," Roxanne said. "And don't come with me to *Bandstand*. Please. Don't. Come," she repeated, drawing out each word for emphasis.

"Me?" Meg gasped. "You think I could get in, too?" Before Roxanne could even respond she answered her own question. "No! Even if I could, I couldn't. I'm supposed to watch Patty at the semifinals."

Roxanne nodded slowly. "Right. So you go watch Patty in her Spelling *B-E-E*—and I'll . . . oh, I'll just dance with the boys on *Bandstand*—Tony deLuca, that cute Jimmy Riley. . . ." She broke into an impromptu scat of "Bandstand Boogie," grabbing Meg for a twirl.

Meg bit her lip. It was awfully tempting. "I don't know," she hedged. "I'll have to ask my dad in just the right way—"

"Meg, we've been waiting on line for the last six weeks," Roxanne pointed out. "How come you didn't worry about your dad before this?"

"Because I never thought we'd actually get in!" Meg shouted. "Okay, I'll ask him tonight."

Thrilled, Meg scooped up her band equipment and school books in one arm, and wrapped

Roxanne in a crushing hug with the other. "We're gonna be on TV!" she exclaimed gleefully. In moments like these, she was delighted that her friend was so much gutsier than she was. Their dreams were finally coming true!

Dinner at the Pryors was chaotic, as usual. Patty was pestering her mother, Helen, Uncle Pete was cracking jokes, and Will was idly pushing a pile of peas on his plate back and forth, biding his time until dessert was served.

"Dad, I have a question—" Meg tried, but to no avail. Her father, Jack, was involved in a heated debate with Meg's older brother, JJ, and his girlfriend, Beth. Meg tried another tack: "Dad, I've got some exciting—" But no one was paying any attention to her. She was starting to wonder if she'd somehow turned invisible.

"Will's using his knife wrong," Patty pointed out.

"I am not," Will protested.

"Could everyone be quiet?" Meg said loudly.

To her surprise, the conversation ceased. She hadn't quite been prepared for everyone to actually *listen* to her. She cleared her throat nervously.

"I just want to say," she continued, aware of everyone's eyes on her, "me and Roxanne—"

"Roxanne and I," Patty corrected.

Meg glared at her. "—are going to dance on *American Bandstand* this Saturday."

"The TV show? No, you are not. Now, could someone pass me the rice?" Jack laid down the law without even missing a beat.

Meg's heart sank. Her father was so quick to dismiss this—didn't he understand how important it was to her? Once he'd made his proclamation, everyone resumed their eating and conversation as though Meg hadn't even announced the most important piece of news she'd ever brought to the dinner table.

"Patty," Helen said, clearly finished with the *Bandstand* discussion, "Grandma knit you a new sweater for semifinals."

Time out, Meg thought with determination. She wasn't going to let this get swept under the rug so easily. Roxanne had gotten them their big break, and Meg wasn't going to squander her opportunity. "Why not?" she asked.

All heads swiveled toward her again, practically in unison.

"Why not?" Meg repeated. "Why can't I go on *Bandstand*?"

"Because I said so," Jack stated, using confounding parental logic.

Normally, Meg would have forced herself to contend with that answer, but not tonight. Not for something like this. "Dad, why not?" she implored. "I do all my homework, all my chores, usually Patty's too, so for once why can't I—"

"Maybe we'll talk about this later," Helen broke in, anxious to keep the peace at the dinner table. Meg felt betrayed by her mother, who was usually so sympathetic.

"We can talk about it till the Phillies win the pennant, but you are not dancing on that show," Jack snapped. He turned to JJ. "So, how was practice today?"

"Why do we always have to talk about football? This is important to me," Meg insisted. JJ was East Catholic's star running back and she was proud of him, but she was tired of the double standard. Jack acted like everything JJ touched was gold: He lived, ate, and breathed JJ's football career. Meg didn't understand why he didn't respect the things that were meaningful to her the way he respected the things that were meaningful to JJ.

"I quit the team," JJ said suddenly.

If Meg thought the table was quiet after her *Bandstand* announcement, she could have heard a pin drop now.

Beth stared hard at her boyfriend, disbelieving. "JJ, you—," she began.

"We talked about this in the summer. Maybe you didn't hear me," JJ started to explain.

"Oh, I heard you," Jack said, fuming. "Now you hear me—you are not quitting that team. So—"

"Too late," JJ said.

"'Too late'?" Jack echoed. "What is going on in this house?" He whirled to face Beth, practically growling at her. "Is this your idea, Beth?"

Beth swallowed hard, offended. "Pardon me?"

"It's got nothing to do with Beth," JJ was quick to assure his father, but Jack was beyond all reason.

"Because some people don't have the kind of money it takes to pay for college," Jack continued. Beth's parents belonged to the country club where JJ waited tables, and their wealth was clearly a bit of a sore spot with Jack. "Some people need the scholarship they get playing football. Even if it's not as classy as getting in on your smarts. Or donating a science lab—"

Beth had heard enough. She pushed her plate aside and rose from the table. "Thank you for dinner, Mrs. Pryor," she said as graciously as she could, and walked out.

"Beth!" JJ called after her. He turned to his father.

"You just don't get it!" he yelled and then ran after Beth.

Carried by the sheer momentum of the conversation, Meg found herself rising from her seat. The fact that her father was giving JJ just as hard a time as he had given her only made her more frustrated. "Yeah. You don't get it!" she shouted.

Then she turned and stalked off to her bedroom.

Meg had been unsuccessful at winning over her parents at dinner last night, but she wasn't willing to give up. Dancing on *Bandstand* had started as a dream, a complete fantasy. But suddenly, it was a dream that was within her grasp. She'd finally get to do something meaningful . . . just as long as she could convince her parents.

Helen was on her hands and knees cleaning up toys Patty had left strewn around the bedroom.

"Mom, he doesn't understand what it means to dance on *Bandstand*," Meg said urgently.

Helen smiled. "And you think I do."

"Isn't there something in your life you wanted so badly that it actually hurt?" Meg asked.

For a second, Helen stopped her cleaning frenzy and gazed straight ahead. She seemed to be lost in thought. "I'll talk with him about it," she agreed when she finally spoke. "But it's still his decision," she insisted.

Meg allowed herself a new ray of hope. "I know," she breathed, "just try. Try really, really hard, okay? Soon as he gets home?" Her eyes twinkled as she pleaded.

"When the time's right," Helen said slowly. "Dad's got a pretty full plate right now."

Meg grinned. It wasn't permission—but it was a start.

"*Ankle socks?*" Roxanne shrieked, taking in Meg's outfit in disbelief. There was no way she would get into *Bandstand* in clothes befitting a Catholic school-girl.

Although Meg's father hadn't come around, and she wasn't normally one for disobeying her parents, Meg had decided she wouldn't be able to live with herself if she didn't take this chance. It was a once-in-a-lifetime opportunity, and she was going to go for it.

Ankle socks or no.

"My parents think I'm studying with you at the library," she explained patiently. "You have to wear socks to the library."

"The socks are the least of our problem," Roxanne announced. "This is a disaster."

"That makes me feel really good," Meg groaned. "Listen, we don't have time to cha—"

"Shhhh. I'm thinking," Roxanne said, cutting Meg off. She scrunched her pretty features into a frown, taking in Meg's outfit in its library-appropriate entirety. "Take off your skirt and top," she said finally. "We'll switch."

Uh, earth to Roxanne—we're at a bus stop here, Meg thought, feeling slightly panicked. Her panic grew as Roxanne proceeded to remove her own shirt. "Here? Now?" Meg cried.

"No," Roxanne said sarcastically. "In your private dressing room at *Bandstand*. Yes. Here. Now."

"Can't we at least use the bathroom?" Meg pleaded.

"You want to miss the bus?" Roxanne asked. Without waiting for an answer, she said, "Take it off."

Wincing, Meg reluctantly started to undress. The bus stop was far from empty, and the other people waiting couldn't help but glance at Roxanne.

Roxanne turned to face the people ogling her. "What? You've never seen a bra before?"

I have to say, Roxanne sure knows how to think on her feet, Meg thought to herself, gazing at her friend with admiration. They now stood on the set of

Bandstand, the clothing switch completed. Roxanne now wore Meg's conservative clothes, looking nothing like the way Meg did in them. "How do you do it?" Meg half-whispered, slightly in awe.

Roxanne gestured to her skirt, not completely satisfied. "It's still a little 'library,'" she complained. "No offense."

The *Bandstand* line guy approached from down the hallway. "So, you happy?" he asked Roxanne.

"Thank you so much," Roxanne gushed, fully appreciative.

"He's cute," Meg commented as he walked off.

"He got us in," was Roxanne's pragmatic reply. Then she exclaimed, "I've got it!" She leaned over and, in one swift motion, ripped the side of her skirt to create a stylish slit.

Meg gasped. "Roxanne!"

"*This* is not too library," Roxanne said with confidence.

Before Meg could argue further, the girls were interrupted by an agitated stage manager. "Are you girls waiting for some kind of engraved invitation?" he demanded. "C'mon!" He waved his arm, and Meg and Roxanne wasted no time in scurrying toward the studio.

* * *

I did it. I'm actually sitting in the bleachers at Bandstand*!* Meg thought. Her heart was beating a mile a minute, she was perspiring, and her throat felt dry. "Are you dying? I'm dying!" she told Roxanne. She meant it. She thought there was at least a 90 percent chance that she had died and gone to heaven.

From her perch in the bleachers, she could see the associate producer, Michael Brooks, standing on the dance floor. He was explaining the taping process for the newcomers. "You new kids, take your cue from the regulars," he explained. "Here we go—lots of energy!" Meg didn't think it was going to be a problem to muster the enthusiasm. In fact, she thought she might burst out of her seat any minute.

"Dibs on Tony DeLuca," Roxanne said. "Jimmy Riley's all yours."

Meg's stomach fluttered. In all the excitement of finally making it onto the set of *Bandstand*, she'd somehow forgotten she was now in direct proximity to the super-adorable Jimmy. What were the chances he'd talk to her? That he'd ask her to dance? Just last week, she would have thought the notion absurd . . . but then again, just last week she was rushing home to watch *Bandstand* in her living room—and today she was dancing on it, live!

As Michael positioned the "Top Ten" list into place, he turned to the stage manager. "Tell Dick we're on in ten."

As the countdown began, the world suddenly shifted into slow motion for Meg. Overcome with excitement, she turned to her friend. "Roxanne, thank you *so* much," she said earnestly. Roxanne smiled and squeezed her hand as the opening notes of "Bandstand Boogie" filled the studio. The show was on.

"Here's your host, Dick Clark!" the announcer boomed, as Dick sauntered gracefully across the stage to pick up the microphone. "Well," he said, speaking to the studio—and to the rest of America—"by now you know our special guests. They are the gentlemen who have released a brand-new record. This song is called 'Don't Worry Baby.' Ladies and gentlemen, the Beach Boys!"

"How's Gina Rizzelli and her big boobs right about now?" Roxanne asked Meg. She had just asked Tony DeLuca to dance for a ladies' choice.

Meg smiled. "I don't want it to end. I just want everything to stop right now. I can't believe we have to go back to our real lives." It didn't seem right, that tomorrow everything was just going to go back to normal. She felt like Cinderella just before the stroke of midnight.

Roxanne nodded. "Tell me about it. 'Cause since we got here, I swear, I'm this close to being Princess Grace."

"Hey, Roxanne," Tony DeLuca called. The girls turned to find him waving from the dance floor. The Ronettes' "Be My Baby" was playing, and he gestured for Roxanne to join him.

"And there's my Prince Ranier," Roxanne sighed, mock put-upon. "Two dances and he thinks he owns me. I already hate this guy."

Meg smiled to herself as Roxanne drifted back into her own fairy tale on the dance floor. She was perfectly content where she was, sitting back and watching the magic happen.

"Would you like to dance?" A distinctly masculine voice broke through Meg's reverie, startling her. She turned around.

Jimmy. Jimmy Riley. Jimmy Riley, the regular on *Bandstand*. Jimmy Riley was standing *right next to Meg*.

And he had just asked her to dance.

Her eyes wide, she quickly blurted, "I would. I'm Meg. Meg Pryor. I go to East Catholic."

"This isn't roll call," Jimmy laughed, cutting her

off. "Just dance with me, Meg Pryor from East Catholic."

She nodded and numbly followed him to the floor.

I am now on the dance floor at American Bandstand. *I am dancing with Jimmy Riley on national television.* Meg was awestruck. All of her dreams had come true in the span of just one hour. She could now die happy.

Jimmy leaned in to her. "I'm gonna turn you so you get some face time on camera two," he whispered. "Ready?"

Meg nodded. She was ready. She'd been ready for this moment all her life.

The cameras had long since been wheeled away, and the kids from *Bandstand*—regulars and newbies alike—were filtering back out into the daylight. Meg lingered, wanting to prolong this experience as much as she could. "Nice to meet you guys, too. Bye," she called after a small cluster of kids.

She floated, mesmerized, to a page taped to the wall of the hallway. She squinted at the blurry print: AMERICAN BANDSTAND—SHOW RUNDOWN NOVEMBER 16, 1963. She ran her fingers across the paper. It was magic, just like everything else at WFIL.

"Take it," she heard from behind her. She whirled around to see Michael Brooks watching her.

Embarrassed, she quickly apologized. "I'm sorry. I didn't mean to—"

But Michael reached past her and pulled the sheet off the wall, handing it to her insistently. "You've got to have something to remember the day you danced on *Bandstand*, right?" he asked.

She nodded. Not that there was any danger of her forgetting about this day. Ever.

"Did you have a good time?" Michael asked.

Is he kidding? Meg thought. "Good? No. That's not the word for it," she said slowly, wanting to capture the exact words to express her feelings. "I mean, I can't imagine anything that'll ever feel so . . . so . . . important. So exactly what I want to do all the time."

"To be on TV?" Michael asked.

"Yeah, on it," Meg agreed. She paused. It was more than that. "But even *around* it. The music, the other kids, Mr. Clark . . . the whole thing." She looked down self-consciously. "That probably sounds silly to you."

Michael shook his head. "No. Sounds a lot like me on my first day. I'm Michael Brooks, the associate producer of the show."

Meg extended her hand. "I'm Meg Pryor."

* * *

"And then he asked for my number," Meg said, telling Roxanne the conversation she'd had with Michael at the end of the taping. She could barely believe it had happened. Outside the windows of the bus, the streets of Philly whizzed by.

"Did you kiss him?" Roxanne asked.

"No, I didn't kiss him," Meg answered, shocked. "He's at least twenty-three. Okay," she said, changing her focus. "We're late because we were at the library studying."

"Actually, we were studying the Battle of Bull Run and the first six weeks of the Civil War," Roxanne clarified. "Good lies are all in the details."

"And we just lost track of time," Meg said.

"And we got so caught up in the 'four score' thing, we switched clothes?" Roxanne asked, pointing to the outfits they'd swapped hours before.

"Oh, my God!" Meg exclaimed. "Hurry!" Without hesitation, she slid out of Roxanne's skirt and shirt while Roxanne peeled off her own borrowed clothing.

Noticing the reaction of the surrounding passengers, Meg mustered up a measure of newfound bravado. "What's the matter?" she asked them. "Haven't you ever seen a bra before?"

* * *

Meg and Roxanne were still laughing when they returned home. Dinner was already in progress, and Meg nervously dug into her prepared speech. "I'm sorry we're late. Smells delicious, Mom."

"We lost track of time at the library," Roxanne added, her face a study of honesty.

Unmoved, Jack glared at the girls. "Maybe you'd like to find out how your sister did at the spelling bee today," he suggested.

Meg couldn't believe she'd almost forgotten. "Oh, Patty," she exclaimed. "How'd you do?"

"I made it to finals," Patty said proudly.

"Of course you did. What was the hardest word you had?" Meg asked, happy for her sister.

"Misandry," Patty said.

"What's that even mean?" Roxanne asked.

"A hatred of men," Patty answered.

"So, you got your studying done?" Jack asked Meg, sounding suspicious.

"Yes," she answered. "We got very caught up in the Battle of Bull Run."

"We did take a short break for lunch. About one-fifteen. I had a tuna melt," Roxanne said quickly.

Are they buying it? Meg wondered when she felt her mother's eyes on her. She looked up to see

Helen eyeing her sockless ankles. She caught Meg's eyes questioningly. *Please, please don't say anything,* Meg begged her mother silently.

The phone rang shrilly, breaking the tension in the room.

"I'll get it!" Patty and Meg offered simultaneously.

"Both of you sit tight," Helen said with finality. "I'll get it."

Jack regarded Meg once more. "You know, Meg," he said, "someone at the store swears they saw a girl who looked exactly like you dancing on *American Bandstand* today."

Oh, no, Meg thought. In all her excitement about dancing on national TV, it had never occurred to her that someone might *see* her dancing on national TV.

Roxanne jumped in. "Well, you know how they say everyone has a twin somewhere in the world."

"How lucky for you, Meg," Jack said dryly, "that your twin happens to be right here in Philadelphia."

"Meg! Telephone," Helen called from the foyer.

Saved by the bell, Meg thought, running off to answer the call. Not that this was going to be the end of the matter.

Her mother stood in the hallway dangling the phone by its cord. "It's a Michael Brooks. From that show you *didn't* dance on today."

Meg knew now that there would be no getting out of this. She sheepishly took the receiver. "Hello?" she asked tentatively.

"Hello, is this Meg Pryor?" Michael asked.

"Uh . . . Michael? Hi . . . ," she said.

"Did you have a good time?" he asked.

"Yes, I did . . . ," she said. *Of course I did.*

"Good, because we'd like you to come back," Michael said.

At first, Meg was certain she'd misheard him. "You want me to what? . . . Oh, God." She was starting to feel sick.

"To come back to *Bandstand* and dance as a regular," Michael repeated firmly.

This isn't a joke. He's really serious. He's inviting me to dance on Bandstand. *As a regular. Just like Tony DeLuca, and Jimmy Riley, and . . .*

The room was spinning. "Ummm . . . could you hold on for one minute?" she asked, as calmly as she was able.

Burying the phone in her sweater to muffle any sound, Meg turned to her mother excitedly. "Mom, I *did* go to *Bandstand* today even though Dad told me not to, but I got to dance with Jimmy Riley, and Michael—he's the associate producer—he just told me that he wants me and Roxanne to come back and dance again. To be regulars. Mom, you have to convince Daddy to let me do this. You just have to." Breathlessly, Meg stopped, awaiting her mother's response.

"You can talk to him yourself," Helen said.

"Please, Mom," Meg begged. "This is the first great thing that's ever happened to me in my whole life." She didn't know what to say to make her mother understand.

"Then I'm sure you'll take care of it first thing," Helen said firmly. "On your own."

"You're grounded," Jack proclaimed, cracking an egg into a glass bowl with precision. He scrambled the egg energetically.

"And I deserve it," Meg agreed, a shade too hastily. "Because I did what you told me not to."

"And then lied about it," Jack added.

"And then lied about it. But they want me to come back to the show," Meg said. She was dressed in her Sunday church clothes.

"I don't care what 'they' want," he argued. "You're grounded. After church I'll decide for exactly how many years. Go talk to Father Kendall and find out how many thousand Hail Mary's you owe for this."

Meg slumped against the kitchen counter.

JJ walked into the kitchen and shot Meg a sympathetic glance. Meg knew her brother was familiar with their father's stubborn streak. Even now, Jack was leveling JJ with a steady gaze.

"We're going to be late," Helen announced, making her way into the kitchen with Patty and Will. Looking at Jack's casual jeans and T-shirt, she added, "I take it you're not joining us for Mass this morning?"

"I'm still working on that chair in the garage," Jack explained.

"That rocking chair's taking longer than the invasion at Normandy," JJ mumbled as he walked out the door.

As Patty, Will, and Helen headed off to greet Father Kendall, Meg and JJ hung back in the church parking lot.

"So," JJ said slowly, "you guys finally got on the show." He knew that Meg and Roxanne had been trying to get on *Bandstand* for months.

"Roxanne," Meg offered, by way of explanation. She wasn't sure quite how to put it.

"Oh," JJ said knowingly. He was aware of Roxanne's reputation, as were most of the students at East Catholic. "Sorry about Dad," he added.

"Me too," Meg agreed. Sorry didn't even begin to describe how she felt.

"Although, I kinda hoped he'd be so mad at you he'd lay off me," JJ said, only half-teasing.

Meg didn't mind her brother's jokes. She knew he'd been bearing the brunt of their father's wrath ever since he'd decided to quit football. "Me too," she said again. "Only, the other way around."

JJ wrapped a brotherly arm around her, and for a moment Meg found that she actually felt a little better. At least she knew that *someone* in her family understood what *Bandstand* meant to her.

Suddenly, a high-pitched voice broke through their special moment. "Meg Pryor! You were on *Bandstand*!" the voice said, half-accusing.

"Gina Rizzelli," Meg whispered to JJ, as Gina raced up and bombarded her with questions. Suddenly, Meg felt very, very popular.

And she didn't much mind the feeling.

The Impressions' "It's All Right" played on Meg's phonograph—good music for sulking. She'd been locked in her bedroom ever since church, crying, and the record was soothing.

If she couldn't bring her father around, she

could kiss her chance to be a *Bandstand* regular good-bye. It was so unfair. Meg thought it was terribly ironic that JJ was not interested in playing football anymore, and Jack was giving him a hard time about it. Meanwhile, she *was* interested in dancing, but her father didn't support it. It just didn't make sense.

She heard a soft knock at the door. "Go away, Patty," she called, dejected.

"It's not Patty." The door opened, and Jack stepped into the room.

"Meg, I'm disappointed in you," he began sternly, standing over her bed. "You defied my authority, then you lied to me about it. I know it was important to you, but that's no excuse."

He paused for a moment, but Meg had nothing to say. Her father was right.

"So you're grounded for two weeks for going to that show without my permission. And you're grounded another four weeks for lying about it."

Meg looked at her father unflinchingly. She knew that she deserved this punishment and wasn't going to protest.

"You can go to school, you can go to church, and you can go to *Bandstand*," her father continued. "And that's it."

Meg nodded. That sounded about right. *School, church, and . . .*

Wait a minute.

Did he just say Bandstand?

Meg's eyes widened as she looked up to see her father grinning down at her. She'd heard him right!

Leaping up from the bed, she threw her arms around him. "Oh, thank you, Dad! Thank you so much!"

"Don't you thank me! I'm punishing you!" he ordered, maintaining his stern composure.

Meg's crying had given way to tears of pure joy. She couldn't hug her father tight enough.

She'd take this punishment, any day.

Meg's life changed irreversibly when her father allowed her to dance on *Bandstand*. Even the drudgery of chemistry class didn't bother her in the slightest. She and Roxanne were holding court, surrounded by a gaggle of uniformed girls dying to hear the details about *Bandstand*. Apparently Gina Rizzelli wasn't the only one impressed by Meg and Roxanne's newfound fame.

"So who else is gonna be on *Bandstand* on Saturday?" one classmate asked over the hiss of the Bunsen burners.

"Besides me and Meg?" Roxanne asked breezily. "Who cares?"

A red-faced student entered the room, flush with news. "It looks like there is some kind of special assembly in the main auditorium," she announced. "The boys are already there."

"What do you think this is about?" Meg asked Roxanne.

"Who cares, as long as the boys are there," Roxanne replied. She smoothed her lips with gloss.

As they were about to head to the auditorium, Father Hayden came into their classroom looking very serious and ashen. Instinctively, Meg reached for Roxanne's hand.

Father Hayden opened his mouth to speak. "I have some terrible news. President Kennedy has been shot."

Suddenly Meg found that she couldn't hear anything. Her senses were stripped raw. At first, the room was silent, processing the news: President Kennedy had been shot.

Assassinated.

Killed.

Then, as the magnitude of the moment dawned on the class, a quiet sort of chaos erupted. Meg wept openly, clutching Roxanne. At that moment, Meg thought that Roxanne's arms were the only thing holding her together. She didn't think she'd ever be able to let go.

Nothing would ever be the same again.

One

If Meg had been listening, she would have heard the sound of rain gently spattering against the roof of the house. But she wasn't focused on anything other than the dull hum of the television set. The low, mournful drone of a funeral dirge played on bagpipes. A Latin Mass was recited in a soothing chant. This was President Kennedy's funeral.

Meg sat on the living-room couch, her vision blurry with tears she didn't bother to wipe away. Her father's arm was wrapped around her; his other arm held tightly to her mother. Helen clutched a tissue and a rosary in one hand and Patty in her other. On the floor, JJ draped a comforting arm around Will. All were rapt, engaged by the subdued activity onscreen. No one in her family had been themselves since they had heard the news.

As the Mass came to a close, an Army band and a Navy choir joined in a quiet tune. While politicians and judges, soldiers and civilians mourned the loss of a hero on television, all of America shared that loss from their own homes. Meg had never felt more united with her country. Under different circumstances, it might have been comforting. As it was, Meg didn't know what she could take comfort in anymore.

"But how do you know they won't cancel it again this weekend?" Gina Rizzelli's voice cut into the air, disturbing Meg's reverie as she stared listlessly at her sewing machine in Home Ec.

Gina was referring to *Bandstand*, of course. It had been cancelled the weekend before—unsurprisingly—but it was scheduled to resume this week.

"Because Dick Clark told Meg and me that Lesley Gore—," Roxanne was saying.

"You don't know Dick Clark," Gina said snidely.

"How jealous is Gina Rizzelli?" Roxanne whispered to Meg. "Answer: very. You know . . ." She trailed off, noticing Meg wasn't really responding.

Meg sighed. "It's weird. We're back at school in Home Ec listening to horrible Gina Rizzelli and it's like nothing even happened. I mean, I know I should feel different, but . . . I don't really."

And that was the problem. The President was dead, and Meg didn't feel any different.

The news had been devastating. Watching the

funeral with her family had been one of the saddest experiences of Meg's life. Her mother was definitely not able to put it behind her; she was still glued to the television set, watching footage from the funeral over and over again.

But for Meg, now that a few days had passed, life went on as usual. And though she felt somewhat guilty, what else was there to do? *School* certainly was carrying on as usual. Even annoying Gina Rizzelli was carrying on as usual.

And *Bandstand*. *Bandstand* was carrying on as usual. Meg found herself wondering, for the first time, if there were more important things than *Bandstand*.

Once the bell rang, Meg and Roxanne made a beeline to the nearest pay phone to call Michael Brooks. "Mr. Brooks?" Meg asked into the phone.

"That's my father. I'm Michael," Michael said.

Meg couldn't help but think he was cute. "It's Meg. Meg Pryor. I'm supposed to dance on *American Bandstand* this Friday."

In the background, she could hear the faint strains of "Locomotion" by Little Eva. Was Little Eva rehearsing in the studio right now? Meg could hardly stand it.

"Yes, Meg, I remember. How can I help you?" Michael asked.

"We were just wondering if—no, I mean—*when*, or really what time we're supposed to be there to do the show. To dance. You know. On *Bandstand*." To Roxanne she whispered, "He thinks I'm an idiot."

"Three thirty. Sharp," Michael said.

"Okay, we'll be there," Meg promised.

"Meg, you keep saying 'we.' Either you're the Queen of England, or there may be a little misunderstanding," Michael said.

Meg suddenly felt a little bit dizzy. Michael had invited her and Roxanne back to the show to dance as regulars . . . right?

Tell me this isn't happening, Meg thought worriedly, rushing down the hallway after Roxanne. "Are you mad?" she asked Roxanne. Roxanne wore an expression of pure indifference, but Meg wasn't so sure it was genuine.

When Meg had been invited back to dance as a regular, she had just assumed that Roxanne was invited back as well. Roxanne was every bit as good a dancer as Meg. And if it hadn't been for Roxanne's . . . er . . . ingenuity, the two of them would have never made it past the line guy to begin with! But Michael

Brooks had told Meg he only wanted her back. Roxanne had said it didn't bother her, but she was tearing down the hall ignoring Meg. *How* was she going to fix this situation?

"'Cause I would be. I'd be mad," Meg admitted, hoping her own confession would get Roxanne to open up. "It's okay," she said, practically pleading with Roxanne to be angry.

Roxanne turned and offered a quick shrug. "No," she said carelessly.

"Maybe I could call him back and ask again," Meg offered, bargaining frantically. "Maybe if—"

"I don't care," Roxanne insisted, and then added with a wry grin, "Bet Gina Rizzelli's gonna get a big kick out of this, huh?" And with that, she stalked off.

No doubt about it, Meg thought helplessly, watching her friend's figure grow smaller and smaller in the distance, *Roxanne is definitely mad.*

Roxanne hadn't come over for dinner the night before, and she hadn't come to the phone when Meg called. But Roxanne couldn't hide forever. Meg hunted her down the next afternoon out by the football field. She wasn't surprised to find Roxanne standing next to the bleachers, sneaking a smoke. She *was*, however, surprised to find Roxanne watching the cheerleaders—specifically Gina Rizzelli—practice.

"I don't know how you guys kick your legs that high in the air, Gina," Roxanne gushed in a saccharine tone. "Not for the life of me."

"Roxanne!" Meg called. "Can I talk to you?"

Roxanne stubbed her cigarette out casually and turned to Gina. "Excuse me one second," she said. With obvious reluctance, she walked over to where Meg stood.

"Gina Rizzelli?" Meg demanded, as Roxanne pulled out another cigarette, lit it, and took a long drag.

"What about her?" Roxanne asked, slowly exhaling a cloud of smoke.

"You said she was a cow," Meg said.

"Sometimes people aren't what they seem," Roxanne countered, with another long exhale. She arched an eyebrow at Meg. "Y'know?"

"This isn't my fault, Roxanne," Meg protested. "I got a phone call from Michael, and he told me—"

"'Michael' who you talked to *privately* after *I* got us on *Bandstand*?"

"But—," Meg cut in.

"And when 'Michael' called to say you were

coming back to be a regular, did you even *ask* about me?" Roxanne asked.

"He didn't bring it up," Meg said quietly. Suddenly, it didn't seem like such a great excuse.

"When I made out with the line guy to get us in, *believe me*, he didn't 'bring you up,' either," Roxanne pointed out. "But I still got us both in."

Why *hadn't* she thought to ask about Roxanne? Meg wondered. Was she a horrible, selfish friend?

No, but in the heat of the moment, she'd gotten flustered. It could have happened to anyone. All she had to do was make things right now. But *how*?

"Roxanne, if they asked you back on the show, and not me—tell the truth—wouldn't you go anyway?" Meg asked. What would Roxanne do if she were in Meg's shoes?

Roxanne paused for a moment. "No, I wouldn't," she said finally.

"You're lying," Meg replied, not believing it.

"I wouldn't go," Roxanne repeated.

"You're only *saying* you wouldn't go because it's not really happening to you," Meg pointed out.

"Roxanne! You've got to see this one," Gina Rizzelli called. "Watch me!"

Roxanne took one last drag on her cigarette. "Do that one where you build the human pyramid!" she yelled. To Meg she said, "They can build a human pyramid." She ground her cigarette out on the ground with the heel of her shoe.

Meg couldn't let the conversation end this way. "Can we talk about this tonight?" she asked.

"I'm having dinner at Gina's house. She's helping me with geometry," Roxanne said.

And with that, she walked away.

Another evening passed without Roxanne joining the Pryors for dinner. Meg couldn't figure out how to resolve the situation. Unless she could somehow change Michael's mind, she just didn't think there was anything that she could do. Hours later, washing up in the bathroom with Patty, Meg scrubbed her teeth with frustration.

Patty leaned over the sink and rinsed her mouth out. "What are you and Roxanne fighting about?" she asked.

Meg never ceased to be amazed by Patty's ability to get to the bottom of any gossip. "Who says we're fighting?" she challenged.

Patty shook her head, wiping away any traces of foam. "Mom asked if you said anything to me about what was bothering you, and I told her that you never tell me anything."

"Thanks," Meg said.

"Because you don't," Patty pointed out.

"That's because it's none of your business," Meg snapped, exiting the bathroom and walking down the hallway toward their bedroom.

Patty scurried along behind her. "Well, if you ever want to tell me, I'd listen," she offered. "And whatever it is, I'm sorry."

Meg stopped in her tracks. "Thanks, Patty," she said softly.

They both went into their bedroom and crawled into their beds. "Well, I think she's wrong," Patty continued, in a much more Patty-ish way. "Roxanne. They want you on the show and not her and so she should—"

Meg shot Patty a look.

"What?" Patty demanded. "You have a very loud phone voice."

Before Meg could even dignify that comment with a response, the girls heard a knock at their door.

Will came in dressed in his pajamas, dragging a sleeping bag behind him. "Can I sleep with you guys until JJ comes home?" he asked. JJ had gone out for the evening with some friends.

"No," the sisters said simultaneously.

"Please?" he begged.

He looked so small and frail, standing there, that Meg had to give in. "All right," she conceded.

"Thanks," he said, laying his sleeping bag flat on the floor and snuggling deep into it. After a moment, he said, "Hey, you guys. You know why he shot him?"

He was referring to JFK, and Meg's heart ached for her baby brother. She knew he was struggling to understand the tragedy, but, unfortunately, no one had an easy answer for him.

"No," Meg admitted.

"Me neither," Will said. "JJ says even Dad doesn't know."

"Politics," Patty said vaguely.

"What's that mean?" Will asked.

"Go to sleep," Patty replied, sidestepping the fact that she didn't know either.

"Hey," Meg whispered to Will. He looked up, and she dropped her hand over the side of the bed to him.

He grabbed on and didn't let go.

The next day, Meg and JJ were in the attic, painting as their mother had asked. It was the last thing she felt like doing, but at least she got to spend some time with her brother. Soon enough he would be off to college, and she'd never get the big brotherly advice that she'd come to rely on.

"JJ," she said tentatively.

"Yeah?" he asked.

"Do you think about it a lot? Or do you sometimes forget about it, like it didn't happen?"

Meg knew she didn't even have to explain what she was referring to—JJ would just get it. And he did. Without missing a beat, he said, "Both. You?"

"I feel bad and then the minute I stop feeling that way, I remember. And then I feel bad because I didn't feel bad." She paused to consider the logic of her words. "I sound like Will."

"I guess it's like Dad said the night of the funeral: You still gotta get up in the morning, go to work, go to school. . . ." He looked at her meaningfully. "Even go to *Bandstand*."

Meg was startled. "What'd Patty tell you?"

"Just that you and Roxanne were having a fight about her not going on the show," JJ said.

"She's such a little spy," Meg fumed. She sighed. "What do I do?"

"Me, I wouldn't go on. You can't let something you want, no matter how bad, get in the way of being a friend. It's not right," he told her.

It wasn't quite the advice she'd been hoping for. "You sound like Dad," she said, knowing he didn't appreciate the comparison. But then she turned to her brother and asked, "Could you give me a ride downtown?"

Usually a buzzing hotbed of pre-*Bandstand* activity, WFIL studio was practically deserted when Meg arrived. The stage was empty, except for Lesley Gore, who was rehearsing for the show. Her voice glided over the closing bars of "You Don't Own Me." As she finished, Meg burst into applause.

"Thank you," Lesley said.

"I'm sorry," Meg apologized, suddenly embarrassed.

"Don't be sorry for liking my song," Lesley said.

"You're Lesley Gore," Meg said, babbling.

"I know," Lesley laughed. "What's your name?"

"Meg. Meg Pryor. Gosh, I am such a big fan. I bought your record the first day it came out, and my sister Patty scratched it, and so my dad made her buy another one for me out of her allowance, but I didn't want to wait till she saved up the money, so I just bought the new one myself." She took a breath. "I can't believe I just told you that story!" she exclaimed.

Lesley laughed again. "It's a good one," she said graciously. "Are you a singer?"

"No. I mean, a little, but no . . . no. I'm not. Definitely not. I'm just a dancer on the show."

"Cool," Lesley said.

"Yeah, cool," Meg echoed, loving the sound of the slang as it fell from her lips.

"I'll make you a deal," Lesley offered. "After the show, you teach me a couple of steps, and I'll give you an autographed copy of my record. Maybe one for Patty, too."

Meg couldn't believe *Lesley Gore* was talking to her as if they were old friends. This was a dream come true. This was what it meant to be a dancer on *Bandstand*.

How was she going to be able to give this up?

"That looked great, Lesley." Meg looked up to see Michael Brooks crossing the dance floor.

"Thank you, Michael. Do you know Meg Pryor? She's a very talented dancer on your show. Sings, too."

Meg thought her face might catch fire, she was blushing so hard. "No, I'm not. And I don't."

"Hi, Meg . . . ," Michael said, glancing at his watch. "While I appreciate your wanting to get here on time, I don't think we need you for four or five hours."

"I know," Meg said.

"Was there something you wanted?" he asked.

Meg paused. She had come to tell Michael that without Roxanne, she didn't think she could be on the show. But now in the studio, making friendly small talk with the likes of Lesley Gore, suddenly, what she wanted was to be on *Bandstand*.

More than anything.

"No, nothing," she said quickly.

"So I'll see you later?" Michael asked.

Meg nodded and hurried off.

"Bye, Meg," Lesley Gore called as Meg left the studio.

Her new friend. Lesley Gore.

What a difference five hours makes! Meg thought excitedly. She was back at the WFIL studio with only two minutes until *Bandstand* was set to air. The studio was alive with activity. Technicians flitted by, yammering into headsets, and nervous dancers chattered away from the bleachers. The bleachers that just last week, Meg had sat in for the first time.

But now she was a regular. And Michael was explaining into a mic, " . . . the regulars will start on the floor for the opening shot."

He meant *her*. Meg could barely contain herself

as the director called out, "Cue theme song. Cue announcer." And as the "Bandstand Boogie" began to play, Charles O'Donnell said, "Welcome to *American Bandstand*. Here's your host . . . Dick Clark!"

Joey Dee and the Starliters launched into a vibrant rendition of "Peppermint Twist," Dick smiling alongside from his perch at the podium. Meg lost herself in the music, feeling completely happy.

All thoughts of Roxanne were forgotten.

After Joey Dee's intro, the curtain parted slightly and Lesley Gore stepped out with her backup singers. Meg watched eagerly from the bleachers. She couldn't believe it when suddenly, Lesley spotted her, smiled, and waved! Lesley really remembered her!

The girl sitting next to her on the bleachers apparently couldn't believe it either. "You know Lesley Gore!" she exclaimed in a stage whisper.

Meg tried to act casual. "Sort of," she said, barely able to contain herself.

"Okay, we *have* to be friends," the girl decided. "Are you here with anybody?"

Meg felt a twinge of guilt. No, she wasn't here with anybody. But she should have been.

"What's your name? My name is Heidi and—"

Meg cut her off abruptly. "Excuse me, can I borrow a pen?"

"All I've got is an eyebrow pencil," Heidi said, producing one from her purse.

Meg found a gum wrapper buried deep in her pocket and scribbled a phone number on it. With grim determination, she headed off to find Michael Brooks.

The door to the Bojarski apartment swung open and Meg found herself face-to-face with Roxanne. It didn't appear that Roxanne was any closer to forgiving her. "What?" she asked, annoyed.

"Rox—," Meg started.

"I saw you on TV," Roxanne said flatly.

"I shouldn't have gone without you," Meg said.

"Too late," Roxanne replied. The damage was done.

The telephone rang and Roxanne ran to pick it up. Meg took a deep breath and followed her into the apartment.

She walked over to Roxanne, who covered the receiver and whispered, "It's Michael Brooks!"

Meg's eyes lit up. Was her plan working?

"This is her—she," Roxanne said into the phone, flushed with excitement. She paused for a moment, listening, then turned to Meg with a frown. "He wants you," she said.

Meg waved her arms madly, gesturing that she wasn't available. Roxanne was more than happy to oblige. "She's not here. May I give her a message?" she said in her most adult tone. After another moment she asked, "What'd she do?"

Roxanne's eyes widened and a smile stretched across her features. "I'll tell her," she said. "But you can count on her to take it very seriously from now on. In fact, I can guarantee she'll be there for the next show.

"And so will I. Bye, Michael!"

The plan had worked. Everything was going to be just fine.

Two

"**I**'m on the list!" Meg nearly shouted. She couldn't believe that after everything she and Roxanne had done to be regulars on *Bandstand*, the line guy was giving them trouble.

She and Roxanne were standing outside WFIL at the front of the long line of hopefuls. Only this time, they were indignant. "See?" Meg said, grabbing his list and pointing a finger at her name triumphantly. "Right there. Meg Pryor."

Roxanne stepped up. "Roxanne Bojarski." She grinned at him. "You must remember me."

The line guy stared at her and turned back to his list. "Sorry," he said. "If you don't appear on the list, you don't appear on the show."

Suddenly, like an angel from heaven, Jimmy Riley appeared. Meg struggled to keep her cool. Jimmy Riley was standing inches from her. She hoped he couldn't hear her heart thumping in her chest.

He was looking right at her, his eyes questioning. "Hi . . . ?" he said.

"Meg Pryor," she filled in. He was talking *to her*.

"Meg Pryor. Meg Pryor from East Catholic. Glad to see you're back," Jimmy said amiably.

Roxanne was still negotiating with the line guy. "Michael personally requested that we—"

Jimmy glanced at the two of them and instantly summed up the situation. "Well, don't waste your time hanging out with this guy," he said. "You're gonna be late. Come on."

He flashed a grin that made Meg melt, and without further ado, the girls were in.

"I can't believe Jimmy Riley remembered my name!" Meg squealed to Roxanne as they tore through the studios.

"Did you see how he was looking at you?" Roxanne countered. "That's not all he remembered."

Standing on the floor, waiting for the final countdown, Meg spotted Jimmy making his way toward her.

"How'd you like to—," he began.

Eagerly, she took a step toward him. *Whatever the end of that question is, the answer is,* yes, I'd love to! she thought.

But before they could connect, Theresa McManus, an older regular, literally pushed Meg out of the way, saying smoothly, "I'd love to." Theresa leaned over to Meg and whispered, "Move," then started dancing with Jimmy.

Meg looked warily to her side. A gawky boy was eyeing her. "Wanna dance?" he asked.

Meg glanced at Theresa, gliding across the floor with Jimmy. She glared in her direction, then turned back to her would-be suitor.

"Sure."

When *Bandstand* ended, Roxanne and Meg reunited on the dance floor to head back to the bus. Feeling a tap on her shoulder, Meg turned to find Jimmy Riley looking down at her.

"Good job out there today, Meg Pryor from East Catholic. Hope we get a chance to dance again," he said.

Meg grabbed Roxanne's arm to prevent herself from fainting dead away. "Really?" she gasped.

"Yeah," Jimmy said easily.

Meg realized Jimmy probably asked girls to dance all the time. *And they probably always say yes,* she thought. So this was no big deal for him. She gathered her composure. "I'd like that," she said, playing it as cool as she possibly could.

Jimmy sauntered off, making room for Theresa to swoop in. "So, you got a crush on Jimmy, huh?"

"No," Meg said, as lightly as possible.

Theresa smiled devilishly. "Don't worry," she promised, "I won't say anything. You seem like a nice girl, so let me give you a little advice: Don't take much of what Jimmy says or does too seriously."

"What do you mean?" Meg asked.

"It's what he does. He likes to 'break in' the new dancers."

Meg wasn't sure what Theresa meant by 'break in,' but she didn't like the sound of it.

After dinner that evening, Meg washed dishes in the kitchen with JJ.

"Was it us?" Meg asked JJ.

The Pryors had just passed an awkward dinner with Sam, the son of Jack's employee, Henry. Henry and his family were colored. Meg had known them all her life, and Henry had always been a loyal employee to her father. She'd never really spent time with Sam, but now, he had gotten a scholarship to run track at East Catholic. And Jack had invited him to dinner to spend time with Meg and JJ, who would be his classmates.

But how would Meg and JJ be able to ease his transition, when they clearly hadn't felt completely comfortable with him at the table? Meg liked Sam well enough and thought he was very nice. It was just that she didn't have any colored friends. There were a few colored dancers on *Bandstand*, but they generally danced with each other, rather than with the white dancers. Meg thought it was stupid that this was the way people behaved. She would have liked to simply be friends with whomever she chose, regardless of their skin color. But somehow, she knew, that wasn't the way the world worked. And dinner tonight had been one more example of that. She didn't understand it, and she didn't know how to fix it.

"I don't know," JJ replied. He didn't deny that the meal had been tense. Sam was going to be running the same events JJ ran; they'd be in direct competition. JJ wasn't used to having any *real* competition when it came to sports, Meg knew. She wondered what that would be like for him.

"Do you think it's strange? That we've never had dinner with Henry and his family?" she pressed.

"Nah, it's just . . . normal," JJ said, drying another freshly washed dish. The phone rang from the hallway. "Besides, I don't think anything's ever the way it's supposed to be," he added.

"JJ," Helen called, "it's Beth."

JJ stopped his drying for a minute, then shouted, "I'll call her tomorrow."

Meg paused to look at her brother, surprised. JJ was crazy about Beth. He *always* took her calls.

"Like I was saying," he said, picking up his washcloth and resuming the dishes.

Sooner or later, everything would change.

A kaleidoscope of dancers fanned across the floor as "One Fine Day" by the Chiffons came to an end. Meg returned to the bleachers to watch Dee Dee Sharp perform the "Mashed Potato."

Jimmy Riley leaned over her, grinning easily. "Why would you name a song this cool 'Mashed Potato'?" he asked her.

Meg shrugged. "Maybe because 'Strained Peas' was taken," she suggested playfully.

"You're funny," he said. "Are you funny on Saturdays, too?"

"What do you mean?" Meg asked.

"I thought we could get together this Saturday," he explained, "and I could see if you're funny then, too."

Meg's heart caught in her throat. "Are you . . . are you asking . . . ," she stammered.

Jimmy smiled, his white teeth gleaming. "Meg Pryor from East Catholic, will you go on a date with me this Saturday?"

Meg was so stunned, she almost forgot to respond. "Oh my gosh, yes. Yes."

"I'll see you soon," Jimmy said. "Saturday."

Meg was cool enough to wait until he'd gone a few paces off before she leaped out of her seat and raced over to where Roxanne was standing.

"What was that?" Roxanne demanded, as quietly as was possible.

"Jimmy Riley asked me out on a date! Roxanne, I'm going on my first date!" The excitement was too much. Meg threw her arms around Roxanne, and the two of them hopped up and down squealing.

Three

After school that afternoon, Meg stopped off at Pryor TV and Radio, her father's shop. She had to ask for his permission to date Jimmy Riley and she was sure his answer would be a definite no. Roxanne had recommended crying, but Meg doubted tears would have the desired effect.

"Hi, hon," Jack greeted Meg as she walked through the front door.

"Hi . . . um . . . Dad . . . ," Meg said, blinking furiously. She was hoping Jack might take it for crying.

"Something wrong with your eyes?" he asked, peering at her curiously.

"No," Meg said quickly, opening her eyes wide. "Um . . . Dad . . ."

"Yes, you can," Jack said, taking Meg by surprise.

"Can what?" she asked.

"Go out on a date with Jimmy Riley."

Seeing Meg's exuberant expression, Jack broke into a grin and continued: "He stopped by about a half hour ago. Asked my permission to take you out. Nice boy."

"He did?" Meg shrieked.

"So here's how it goes," Jack said, suddenly sounding businesslike. "He picks you up at the house, he meets your mother, and you take *the bus* to the movies—no car."

"I love the bus!" Meg trilled.

"And you're home by ten."

"Ten?"

"Nine forty-five," Jack amended.

"What?"

"Nine-thirty," he said. "You want to try nine?"

"Okay, okay," Meg agreed hastily. "Ten."

"Nine-thirty," Jack corrected. "Sharp."

She threw her arms around her father, unable to contain her excitement. "Thank you, thank you, thank you," she said, repeating the phrase as though the words were magic.

Suddenly, Meg heard a familiar voice. From the television set behind her she heard, "Next on WFIL . . . in just five minutes . . . *American Bandstand*! Today's guests include . . ."

"Oh, my gosh!" Meg shouted. "I have to go!"

"Nine-thirty!" Jack called as she dashed off in the direction of the studio.

But Meg was already gone.

* * *

"Why are all your clothes so . . . high school?"
Roxanne moaned, assessing the contents of Meg's
closet. Meg had realized that securing her father's
permission to go was just the first step. She had *no
idea* how to behave on a date! That was where
Roxanne came in.

"So, after dinner, if he offers you gum, take it,"
Roxanne instructed. "It means he wants to make
out."

Meg bit her lip nervously. "You think he will?"

"If he's alive," Roxanne said. She didn't seem to
think it was going to be an issue.

Meg couldn't believe how casually Roxanne was
handling this. Didn't she understand the magnitude
of Meg's very first date? And possibly her very first
kiss? And that this was all going to happen with the
extremely adorable Jimmy Riley?

"If he takes you to see a scary movie, that's
good," Roxanne continued. "It means he wants to
protect you. Put his arms around you."

"What am I going to talk about?" Meg wondered
suddenly.

Pulling a skirt from a hanger, Roxanne said, "This is
hideous." She turned back to Meg. "That's the beauty of
a movie. No talk. You only have to talk during dinner.
Which you don't eat. Not one bite. You could get food

stuck in your teeth." She pulled another skirt from the closet. "This is cute . . . sort of . . ."

"What do I talk about?" Meg repeated. Roxanne hadn't really gotten around to answering that question.

"He's a guy. Talk about cars."

Cars? Meg wondered. *What do I know about cars?*

"The main thing with boys is, you've got to make them feel smarter than you. About everything," Roxanne said, as though this information were common knowledge.

"How do you do that?" Patty asked, from her perch on her bed.

"Get out!" Meg shouted, crossing the room and opening the door.

"If you tell me about making boys feel smart, I'll tell you the reason JJ isn't going to Beth's mixer," Patty said knowingly. "He's embarrassed 'cause he can't dance."

"He can so," Meg countered.

"Have you ever seen him?" Patty pointed out.

"I've never seen you get out, but I know you can," Meg replied.

In one swift movement, she shoved Patty back out into the hallway.

*   *   *

Later that night, Meg changed into her pajamas and crept down to the kitchen where JJ was studying. She crossed to the refrigerator, poured herself a glass of milk, and sat down at the table next to him.

"What are you doing?" she asked softly.

"Chemistry," JJ replied. "You're so lucky you'll never have Father Clarke," he mumbled. Science wasn't JJ's best subject.

Meg gestured to the transistor radio on the kitchen counter. "Can I change this?" she asked, and then got up and fiddled with the radio until she found a station playing "Somewhere Over the Rainbow" by Judy Garland.

"I love this old song," she said. "Remember when we saw this movie and Will was so scared of the flying monkeys?"

"I'm still scared," JJ said, laughing.

Meg stood up and executed a few dance moves, imagining a partner was leading her. She hummed along quietly to the music as she moved.

JJ watched her curiously. "Where'd you learn how to dance?" he asked.

She smiled at him. "I just taught myself," she said. She put out a hand to him.

JJ shook his head. "Nope, forget it," he said.

"Oh, come on," Meg insisted, taking his arm and

dragging him to his feet. She positioned him properly to lead and began to run through some basic dance steps. "Slow, slow, quick-quick, slow," she said, as he rocked awkwardly. "Slow, slow, quick-quick slow . . ."

"Slow, slow, quick-quick, slow," JJ intoned in sync with her. He began to match his steps to her own.

And before the end of the night, Meg had taught her older brother to dance.

It was funny, Meg thought, how all the anticipation of the past few days didn't make it any easier to believe she was, at last, getting ready for her date with Jimmy Riley. She was so nervous she thought she might not be able to go through with it. Ever since she'd been about ten years old, she'd been imagining her first date. But she never in her wildest dreams imagined her first date would be with someone who was practically a celebrity. She thought she might be the luckiest girl in the world.

That was, she *would* be the luckiest girl in the world if she could bring herself to go through with the date. Her hands were shaking as she ran a brush through her thick blond hair.

She was startled by a knock at the door. "Go away, Patty!" she called.

"It's not Patty," said JJ, stepping through the door.

"I'm trying to get ready, JJ," Meg protested.

"I know. I just thought—I figured I oughta—it being your first date and all . . ." JJ's voice trailed off. He sat down on the edge of her bed. "So . . . ," he said uncomfortably, "have a good time."

"Okay," Meg agreed.

He sighed and retreated to the door. "And be careful," he warned.

"I will," Meg assured him.

JJ leveled her with a steady gaze. "And don't take any, you know, garbage from him. From anyone," he continued. "Ever. Okay?"

Meg was silent, touched by her brother's concern.

"Say, 'okay,'" JJ instructed.

Meg smiled. "Okay," she said.

If Meg thought JJ was having a hard time coping with her first date, she certainly wasn't prepared for how emotional her mother became. "Meg, I wanted to—," she began, walking into Meg's room. She stopped when she saw Meg, dressed and waiting. "Oh, Meg," she said, tears welling in her eyes. "You look beautiful."

"Really?" Meg asked. She hoped her mother wasn't just saying that.

"I wanted to lend you Grandma's locket," Helen told Meg. She gently lifted Meg's hair off of the nape of her neck and clasped the necklace in place.

"My mouth is dry, I'm sweating, and I feel like I might throw up," Meg confessed.

"You're just nervous," Helen said. She stepped back, looking at Meg once more. The tears in her eyes threatened to spill over.

Meg groaned. "Mom," she protested, rolling her eyes.

Helen laughed. "I can't help it," she said.

Deep inside, Meg didn't really mind at all.

Cars. Roxanne said boys like cars, Meg reminded herself as she and Jimmy got off the bus and headed into the movie theater. Ever since they'd left the house, she'd been wracking her brain for any car-related anecdote. Easier said than done. Even with an older brother around the house, Meg hadn't had very much exposure to cars. She hoped that the enthusiasm in her voice would make up for her relative lack of knowledge. "It was a '51 Chevy Hemi with a B-8 engine," she said, picking up a conversation that had begun during dinner.

"You mean a V-8?" Jimmy asked.

"Right!" Meg agreed. She could hear the energetic lilt to her voice. It wasn't exactly natural, but she wasn't sure how to bring her tone back down. "My dad bought it when I was four. You could pop out the windshield. I don't really know why you'd want to pop out the windshield and we never did, but my dad seemed excited."

Oh god, she thought. *Someone please save me from myself.*

"Meg, are you okay?" Jimmy asked.

"Oh, yeah," she said, nodding vigorously.

"No, I mean—you haven't stopped talking since we left your house. Even at dinner. Plus, you didn't eat a thing."

"I guess I'm not hungry," Meg said uncertainly. Jimmy didn't say anything. When the silence became unbearable, Meg jumped in again. "I love your jacket," she said. "You look really good in green."

"My sister told me to wear it," Jimmy said. "I hate green."

Well, at least it's a scary movie, Meg thought. They were going to see *The Birds*.

"You like scary movies?" Jimmy asked.

"Love them," Meg replied, smiling. *Especially if*

you'll hold me during the scary parts, she thought.

As they walked past the concession stand, Meg saw Henry's son Sam wiping down the counter. He was wearing a uniform. Meg still felt a little bit uncomfortable seeing Sam, even now. But she decided she'd have to put the dinner behind her if she wanted things to be normal between them. "Sam?" she asked tentatively. "What are you doing here?"

"I work here," he replied.

"Sam, this is Jimmy Riley," she said.

"I know who you are," Sam said to Jimmy. "I've seen you dance on *Bandstand.*"

Even under these circumstances, Meg couldn't help but feel a slight thrill that someone recognized her date from TV. "Sam's dad works for my dad," she explained to Jimmy.

"Cool," Jimmy said easily. "Have you seen the movie yet?"

"Thirty-four times. Hold onto your seats," Sam warned them.

Meg nearly shuddered with anticipation. She might have to do just that!

Sam was right, the movie was a nail-biter. A small town was overrun with evil birds that would peck to death anything in sight. Between the movie and the proximity of Jimmy, Meg was terrified.

She sat stiff as a board, her eyes glued to the screen, but inside her head she was only focused on Jimmy. She could feel his breath on the side of her face. He had casually draped his arm across the back of her chair—and she waited to see what, if anything, his next move would be. *What will I do if he tries to kiss me?* she wondered. She was torn between hoping he wouldn't and praying he would.

On screen, a woman crept up the stairs of the attic. Meg's heart pounded.

"Gum?" Jimmy asked her abruptly.

Meg flinched and knocked the pack of gum to the ground. "Sorry," she said, mortified.

"That's okay," Jimmy said, reaching down to pick the pack up.

Meg thought her heart might actually explode. The gum could only mean one thing: her first kiss!

But then the woman in the movie opened the attic door and was attacked by a fierce pidgeon. Meg jumped out of her seat—just in time to smash Jimmy in the face with her elbow.

"Ow," Jimmy cried, clapping his hands over his nose. A thin trail of blood trickled through his fingers.

Oh no, I've clobbered my date, Meg thought wildly.

"I think I'm bleeding," Jimmy moaned. He stood and began to climb over the other audience members. "Excuse me," he said, stepping clumsily down the aisle.

Meg followed on his heels, mumbling "Excuse me," as she tiptoed out, thoroughly embarrassed.

"It's not pretty," the theater manager assessed as he, Meg, and Sam helped to clean Jimmy up. "Nothing's broken, but it's swelling badly. Has the bleeding stopped? Nope," he answered his own question quickly.

"You're gonna have a real shiner," Sam said.

"You should get right home and lie down. Sam, get him some ice," the manager said.

Jimmy turned to Meg. "I'll walk you home . . . ," he began.

"No," Meg insisted. "Don't worry about me. My dad'll come get me. You should go. Do we call an ambulance—"

"I'll be fine," Jimmy said, laughing. At least *he* could still laugh at this situation.

"Um, Jimmy," Meg said, as he put on his jacket and prepared to head home, "thanks for . . . I mean . . . I had a really good time."

"Yeah," Jimmy said quickly. "Me too."

* * *

After Sam finished sweeping up and cleaning the concession stand, Meg still stood alone in the movie theater. The manager left, too, and suddenly Meg was self-conscious. Where was her father?

Sam stood at the door of the theater, looking at Meg. She could tell he felt bad about leaving her. "Patty said she'd tell him as soon as he got home. My dad," Meg said. She didn't want him to feel like he had to wait with her. "I can't imagine where they'd be so late." She rubbed her arms as if to stave off a chill. "You probably have to get home. I guess I better . . . I'll just walk."

Sam looked as though he didn't think that was the best idea. "I'll walk you," he offered tentatively.

"Okay," Meg said. It was very dark outside, and it wasn't a short walk home. They left the theater together and started down the street.

"Was this your first date with him?" Sam asked.

"Him? First date, period. Ever."

"It probably seemed worse than it was," Sam said.

"You think so?" Meg asked. She sure hoped so.

"Sure. It was probably the blood that threw you," Sam teased.

Meg smiled. "Probably."

Suddenly, a police car stopped at the curb. A bright light shone from the car, washing across their faces.

"Step away from that girl, young man!" boomed a voice from inside the car. "Miss? You all right?"

Meg raised her arm to shield her face from the blinding light. *Of course she was all right.* "Yes, fine," she said.

"You know this boy?" the cop asked.

"Yes," Meg said. "I got left at the movie theater. He's walking me home."

"You're walking this girl home?" the officer asked Sam skeptically.

"Yes," Sam said quietly.

"What's your name?" the officer demanded.

"Sam Walker," Sam said.

Meg was shocked. She knew that lots of people were prejudiced, but this was the first time she'd ever seen it firsthand. And to a friend of hers—all because he was doing her a favor! She wished there were something she could do or say to make it better.

"You're *sure* you're all right?" the cop asked Meg again.

"She's fine, officer."

Meg was flooded with relief at the sound of her

father's voice. But when she turned to see him, she could tell he wasn't very sympathetic to her situation.

"I'm Jack Pryor, Pryor TV and Radio, over on Sixth," Jack said. "My brother Pete's over at the Columbia Avenue precinct. This is my daughter Meg. And Sam Walker. His father works for me," he explained.

"Okay, Mr. Pryor," the officer said. It infuriated Meg how quickly the cop accepted Jack's explanation, but gave Meg and Sam such a hard time.

"I appreciate your stopping," Jack said. Meg was appalled. The cop hadn't been doing them a *favor* by stopping—he'd been harassing Sam!

"Sam, go home. Meg, get in the car."

There was no arguing with the tone in Jack's voice. Without saying good-bye or even looking at Meg, Sam turned and walked off.

"What were you *thinking*?" Jack roared, once they were home.

Meg couldn't understand her father's reaction. "What should I have done? Walked home by myself?"

"Sam's a good boy. You put him in a bad situation," Jack said. "Do you realize what could have happened out there?"

Meg thought about the policeman and how suspicious he'd been. It could have gotten a lot uglier. She just hadn't thought about that possibility. "We weren't doing anything wrong," she insisted. "You don't get it."

"You're right," Jack agreed. "I don't. Go to bed."

As she was leaving school the next day, Meg saw Sam getting ready to walk home. She knew that he saw her as well. They made eye contact briefly, and then slowly dropped their eyes, lowered their heads, and moved off in opposite directions.

Four

"**H**ow could anyone hate you?" Roxanne asked. They were in their usual seats in the *Bandstand* bleachers, and Meg was fretting over her fiasco with Jimmy Riley.

"I gave him a black eye, Roxanne," Meg said. "I mean, they had to shoot him in profile three days in a row. And if that's not—"

"Hey, Cassius!" called Jimmy. Amazingly, he didn't seem angry at all.

"Jimmy . . . ," Meg said tentatively. "Hi."

"Oh, look at the time," Roxanne exclaimed, the picture of subtlety. "I should have been flirting with that Best Boy fifteen minutes ago."

Meg flashed her friend a *don't you dare leave me here alone look*, but Roxanne grinned and darted off. Meg looked at Jimmy's face. The bruise *had* healed quite a bit. "Your eye looks a lot better," she offered lamely.

Jimmy nodded. "Cold compress," he said.

"Oh, great," Meg commented. "Cold compress.

They're great. Really . . . the cold . . . with the compressed . . ." She trailed off when she realized she had no idea what she was talking about.

"Actually, there's something I wanted to ask you," Jimmy said.

"Me? Sure, anything," Meg said, eager to find a new topic of conversation.

"Sixty seconds, people," the director shouted, cutting them off before Jimmy could ask.

"Find me at the first commercial break. We'll talk then," Jimmy said, and rushed to take his place.

Meg had no idea how dandruff could ever be considered romantic, but the first commercial to play during *Bandstand* was a surprisingly romantic commercial for dandruff shampoo. Or, maybe it wasn't surprising. Maybe this was how she was going to see *everything* from now on. Through rose-colored glasses. Because when she'd finally gotten to Jimmy and had a chance to talk to him, he'd asked her if she wanted to be a couple!

She still couldn't believe her ears. "Like Randy and Joanne? On the show?" she asked breathlessly.

"Like Randy and Joanne," Jimmy agreed. "Although personally I think we'd be better. Because we're us, you know."

Meg could do little more than stare at Jimmy. "So we'd be a couple," she repeated, drunk with the thought.

"Why don't we meet here Thursday. After school. To practice," he said.

Better yet, let's just stay right here until then! "I'd love that. I mean, okay. I will. I can," Meg stammered.

"Just to make sure we have rhythm together. But I'm betting we do," Jimmy said.

Meg nearly swooned. "Yeah, me too," she replied.

The next day, Meg and Roxanne were hanging out at the Vinyl Crocodile, their favorite record shop. Meg was rehashing her conversation with Jimmy. "Do you really think he does? Or not really?" she pressed.

"Meg," Roxanne said sternly, "Jimmy Riley has been blessed with one of the great pickup lines of our time—'Will you dance with me on *Bandstand*?'— and he's not gonna waste it on someone he isn't crazy about. Face it, he's got it bad."

Meg didn't care if Roxanne was only telling her what she wanted to hear. It was worth it.

Taking note of the clerk behind the counter, Roxanne unbuttoned her top button. "Hold on. I need to remind Adam how much he likes me." As she crossed over to where Adam was working, she noticed Sam come out of the listening booth. "Hi, Sam," she said, breezing past him.

Meg glanced quickly at Sam. She hadn't spoken to him since the disastrous night at the movie theater. She'd never even had a chance to thank him for the gesture . . . or to apologize for the fact that he'd been given so much trouble for it. At a complete loss, she finally managed, "Sam. Hi. I didn't see you."

Noting her discomfort, he jumped in. "I was in the listening booth."

"Good?" Meg asked, pointing to the record in his hand.

He made a face that suggested otherwise, but said nothing. "Anyway," he said finally, "I'm late for track, winter practice, so—"

"Okay," Meg said, a bit relieved. "Bye, Sam."

"Yeah," he said. "See you."

With a small wave, Meg watched him leave the store. There really wasn't anything else for her to say.

On Thursday, Meg met Jimmy at the WFIL studio to see about their rhythm. "It's great we get to be here alone," she said, as the sound tech cued up some music for them. "To practice, I mean." Meg smiled at him, unsure of what to say next. Fortunately, she was saved as "Rhythm of the Falling Rain" by the Cascades gently filled the studio. The song was slow and romantic, and Meg found herself brimming with anticipation. "I love this song," she said.

"I saw them at the Palestra last year," Jimmy said. "Here, lemme . . ." He arranged Meg in the proper position, then stepped in and took her hands, leading her. They began a bit awkwardly, but soon found their rhythm. Meg wasn't sure what to say, or if she was even supposed to talk. It didn't matter. She was completely content to dance with Jimmy. As they glided around the room, Meg found she was able to put her own spin on Jimmy's moves. He was right. They weren't just good together.

They were *great*.

Practice was one thing. Now Meg was ready for the real thing. She primped at the WFIL makeup table, making a few last-minute adjustments before *Bandstand* taped.

Roxanne noticed her tugging at her skirt. "Relax, he's *already* crazy about you. He picked *you*, Meg—and . . . he's right behind you," she whispered pointedly. "Hi, *Jimmy*," Roxanne said loudly.

"Hi," Jimmy said.

"Oh, hi," Meg said, regaining her composure.

Jimmy swept his gaze across her admiringly. "Wow. You look . . ." He let his voice trail off.

"Thanks," Meg said. "You, too. You know," she said nervously, "my brother plays for East Catholic. Football. Well, he quit the team, but now he's playing again. He wants to get a scholarship to Notre Dame. Anyway, after his games, we get ice cream sometimes. My family does. At Burrell's on City Line. And if you're not doing anything . . ." Meg stopped talking midsentence when she realized that Jimmy was looking at her strangely. "Just to meet my family again," she said uncertainly. "You only met them once, but if you can't, that's no big—"

"Meg," Jimmy interrupted, "you know why I asked you to be a couple, right?"

"Sure," she replied brightly. "Of course. Because . . ." She stopped again. All of her confidence left her. "No," she admitted. "Maybe I don't. Why did you?"

"Because Michael Brooks thought we looked good together," Jimmy said. He said it simply, as a mere statement of fact. As though he wasn't actually shattering her heart into a million small pieces with one offhand remark. "He's real good at that stuff, Michael. Putting two people together."

"But you said . . . you said, just like Randy and Joanne," Meg said.

"Right, exactly. If we're lucky." Jimmy stopped and looked hard at Meg, realizing how badly she had misread the situation. "Meg, do you think Randy and Joanne are a *real* couple?"

Meg's silence was answer enough.

"Joanne's engaged to a merchant marine," he said. "Randy's got a girlfriend in the tenth grade. They're dance partners. That's it. All that 'couple' stuff is just for the fans."

Meg shook her head, trying to make sense of his words. She couldn't admit what she was really thinking.

It wasn't just for the fans, Jimmy, she wanted to say. *It was for me.*

"But the date," she stammered. "I know it wasn't perfect, 'cause of the black eye. And the blood. But when you called me 'Cassius,' I thought—"

"The date was fine, Meg," Jimmy assured her.

"Fine?" Meg repeated.

Jimmy nodded. "Honest. But it's better this way. No feelings to make things all weird. Just partners. And friends."

The word "friends" hit Meg like a slap in the face.

"So what do you say, Meg? Friends?" Jimmy

asked her. She could hear the director counting down. She had to pull herself together. Any minute now, she was going to be on live TV.

As "Bandstand Boogie" cued up, Dick Clark announced, "Let's start things off with our Spotlight Dance and *Bandstand*'s newest couple, Meg and Jimmy, dancing to the Cascades and 'Rhythm of the Falling Rain.'"

As Meg and Jimmy took center stage, she sadly realized that her dreams were finally being played out. Just like she'd fantasized, she was dancing with Jimmy as his partner. They were a couple. It was just like her dreams.

But, just like her dreams, this moment wasn't real.

Five

When Meg and Roxanne weren't racing off to *Bandstand* after school, they hung out at the Vinyl Crocodile and listened to records. One afternoon, Dusty Springfield's smooth vocals were playing on the store's phonograph, until Roxanne bust into the room and lifted the needle from the record.

"You won't believe what happened!" she said as Dusty came to a screeching halt.

"Roxanne, I was listening to that!" Meg said, annoyed.

"Easy on the vinyl," she heard someone say. "You scratch it, you buy it."

Luke. Luke Foley was a high school student who worked at the Vinyl Crocodile. He was kind of cute, in a very offbeat sort of way, with thick, dark, unruly hair and Buddy Holly glasses. He was very into folk music and not at all appreciative of the acts normally showcased on *Bandstand*. It was clear he thought Meg was some kind of cultural moron for not liking Bob Dylan.

Meg handed Luke her 45s so he could ring her up. Seeing which single she'd selected, he shook his head. "It never fails. Mr. Greenwood puts a Top Forty on and every lemming . . ." Realizing what he had just said, he awkwardly stopped speaking.

Unfortunately, the words were already out. "Every *what*?" Meg asked.

"Every*one* buys it," Luke amended, too late.

"This is a record store, isn't it?" Meg pointed out, snidely. "Where you buy records?"

"Sure," he said offhandedly. "Sixty-nine cents, please."

She fumbled through her change purse, counted out the right amount, and snatched her bag from him angrily. "And I am *not* a lemming!" she snapped.

Meg marched to the front door. "Roxanne!" she said, indicating that it was time to go. When Roxanne caught up to her, Meg leaned close and whispered, "What's a lemming?"

The next day, Meg went back to the Vinyl Crocodile. She arrived just as Luke was turning the sign from OPEN to CLOSED. She tapped on the window. He pointed to the sign.

Meg pushed the door open anyway. "You gave me the *wrong* record!"

"Yeah, I know," he admitted. "I've got to lock up."

"What do you mean, you *know*?" she demanded. "You gave me this . . . this Bob Dylan on *purpose*?"

"I just thought you might want to listen to something . . . ." He struggled to find the right words. ". . . better."

Meg fumed. "And what, may I ask, is wrong with *my* song?"

"Hmmm," Luke said, considering. "Let's start with the lyrics. 'My boyfriend's back and you're going to be in trouble,'" he deadpanned.

"That song is Top Ten!" Meg shouted.

"Exactly," Luke agreed.

"Wait, wait," Meg protested. "'In the jingle jangle morning I'll come follow you'? What exactly is a 'jingle jangle morning'?"

"You're making fun of Dylan?" he asked with disbelief.

"Is that different from the 'bingle bangle morning'? And how about his voice? He sings like . . . well, he can't sing!" she finished emphatically.

"'Hey la, hey la, my boyfriend's back,'" Luke sang dryly.

That did it. "Can I have my record, please?" Meg asked. As he bagged her single she said, "It just so happens I like the Angels, Mr. Bob-Dylan-Felonius-Monk."

"Thah," Luke said. "It's *Thelonius. Thah*, not *Fah*."

She snatched the bag from his hands and stormed off.

After *Bandstand* the next day, Meg returned to the Vinyl Crocodile once again. "You did it *again*. You deliberately gave me Bob Dylan *again*," she seethed.

Luke didn't bother to look up from the shelves. In fact, Meg could swear he seemed amused by her annoyance. "Did you listen?" he asked.

"No, I didn't," Meg answered. "I told you I don't like him."

"How do you know if you don't even listen? What do you know—"

"I know about music!" Meg insisted. "I dance on *American Bandstand*."

Luke laughed derisively. "You know *dancing*, not music."

"Fine!" Meg said, frustrated. "I'll listen to your stupid record, if you listen to mine!"

"Sure, let's go," he agreed, calling her bluff and leading her to the listening booth.

Uh-oh. Meg certainly hadn't expected him to agree! "Now? I can't," she said.

"Right," Luke said, not believing her.

Defensively, Meg pointed to her watch. "The Catholic League Championship. I have to play."

"You play football?" Luke asked sarcastically.

"I play in the band," she said.

Luke smiled. "I had a hunch. Lots of John Phillip Sousa." He hummed a few bars, miming a band conductor.

Meg was charmed despite herself. She laughed. "I don't choose the songs."

"So we finally agree on something," Luke said.

"Why aren't you going?" Meg asked, letting her guard down ever so slightly. "Oh, don't tell me . . . you probably don't like football, right?" He probably didn't like anything as traditional and all-American as sports.

"No, I love football," Luke said, surprising her. "I told Mr. Greenwood I'd work so he could go. He likes football, too."

Meg found herself almost disappointed.

"So, are you going to listen?" Luke asked her, indicating the Dylan 45.

Meg shrugged. "I can only buy one this week."

"My treat," Luke said. "Promotional copy." And then he bagged *both* 45's.

Leaving the store, Meg wondered why Luke had

given her a 45 for free. Why did he care so much about what she listened to? And more important, why did *she* care about his opinion?

Six

Days passed, and soon enough the City Championship game was upon the students of East Catholic High. If Meg had been preoccupied by her feelings about Luke—which were mostly limited to annoyance—she didn't have time for that anymore. The school library was silent when Meg and her bandmates burst in in full uniformed regalia, playing their hearts out to "The Saints Go Marching In."

The band members finished their number and stepped aside to make way for the cheerleaders. "We are Crusaders, Mighty Crusaders. Everywhere we go, people want to know, who we are, so we tell them," they chanted, before launching into the same verse all over again.

"I don't think anybody *really* wants to know who those girls are, do you?"

Meg whirled around, startled, to find Luke standing right next to her. Just when she had managed to get him out of her mind, here he was, bothering her. "Maybe you're just not a fan of school spirit," she snapped.

"Of course I am," Luke argued. "Especially when I get to listen to fine marching music and people spelling at the same time."

"Then I guess it's a good thing you're easily entertained," Meg replied.

"Yeah, I am," he agreed. "Your hat, for instance, I find very entertaining."

He grinned and walked to the library desk, leaving Meg to glance self-consciously at her conspicuous headwear and glare in his wake.

Meg thought the one place where she could get away from Luke would be her home. But after school that evening, she answered the doorbell—only to find Luke standing on her doorstep.

"Hello, Meg," Luke said.

"Now you're coming to my *house* to make fun of me?" she asked.

"Well, if you want to go put on that red hat . . ." He trailed off, seeing her lack of amusement. "I'm actually here to give a piano lesson to"—he glanced at a crumpled piece of paper—"Patricia Pryor."

"What happened to Mr. Porter?" Meg demanded. This could *not* be happening. Luke was *not* coming to her house, now, to give Patty piano lessons.

"I'm muscling into his territory," Luke joked.

Meg didn't crack a smile. "Really."

"Dislocated hip," Luke explained.

"And you play piano?"

"I find it helps with the teaching," he said with his usual sarcasm.

Much to Meg's chagrin, it turned out that Luke was pretty good at the piano. *Okay, more than 'pretty good,'* she thought grudgingly. *Very good.* Sitting next to Patty at the piano bench, he demonstrated some finger arrangements, then plucked out some chords on his own.

"Stand By Me," Patty said, recognizing the tune. "Why are you teaching me *this* kind of song?"

"Because this is the kind of music you'll *want* to practice," Luke said patiently. "Here, let me." He slid farther down the bench and played some of the trickier notes.

Meg glanced over at Roxanne, who had arrived shortly after Luke. She was swaying in tune to the music, clearly charmed. "He thinks he's so great," Meg grumbled.

"He is, kinda," Roxanne replied.

Meg sulked, not sure which one of them annoyed her more.

The next day at WFIL, Meg arrived to find Roxanne clutching a pay phone receiver and chatting into it softly, engrossed. Given the small smile on her face and the flirty tone to her voice, Meg had to assume that her friend was talking to a boy. But who?

She hung up. Meg looked expectantly at her friend. "Okay. Who were you talking to?" she asked.

"Nobody," Roxanne said simply.

"You were using your 'boy' voice," Meg insisted. "Just tell me."

"Okay, okay," Roxanne said, caving. "It's not that big a deal. I was talking to Luke."

This was the last person Meg was expecting Roxanne to be interested in. "For what?" she asked suspiciously.

"He wants me to come by the store and listen to some new records they just got in."

"Oh," Meg said. That didn't sound so romantic. But the way Rox was talking on the phone . . . "It just sounded so . . . He made you promise that you'd come? Luke?"

"I guess he's just excited about the new records," Roxanne said.

"Why didn't you tell me?" Meg asked.

Roxanne thought for a moment. "I mean, *you* don't like him, do you?" she asked.

"No. No," Meg said emphatically. "Of course not."

* * *

If there was one thing that was *almost* as annoying as Luke Foley, it was geometry. The next day at school, Meg tried to explain it to Roxanne.

"Okay, here's what I don't get about an isosceles triangle," Roxanne complained. "Everything."

"Just remember two of the sides are the same length," Meg explained, pointing with her pencil to the diagram in her math book. Unfortunately, she couldn't stop thinking about Roxanne's evening with Luke. Trying to sound casual, she asked, "So what happened to you last night?"

"Luke had to get the store ready for a performance. Some folk music girl. So I stayed to help." Turning back to the geometry textbook, Roxanne continued, "Why do *I* need to prove Pythagorus's theory? If it's not true, why'd they put it in the book?"

"It couldn't have taken that long," Meg mused, "setting up with Luke."

"Well, then he couldn't resist playing me some more music."

Meg's stomach turned over. "What kind of music?" she asked, wanting but not wanting to know.

"The kind he made you listen to," Roxanne said.

Meg felt sick. "Bob Dylan? He played Bob Dylan for you?"

"He's a poet," Roxanne said. Meg must have looked confused, because she quickly clarified, "Bob Dylan. Not Luke. But Luke is so, so . . . interesting. And smart. And funny. Did you know he was funny?"

"I hadn't really noticed," Meg said.

"He's different from other guys," Roxanne said. "Like those East Catholic jocks or those college guys we talked to on the bus. And guess what . . . he asked me to go out tonight."

Meg wasn't going to miss the championship game, even if Roxanne wouldn't be there next to her. As she searched the house for her clarinet, the doorbell rang. Meg opened the door to find Luke standing on the front steps.

"Hi," Luke said. "I'm just here to drop off some sheet music I promised Patty."

"I'm surprised you were able to find the time," Meg said. "With your busy social schedule and everything."

Luke looked puzzled by her tone of voice.

"He's dead!" Will's voice echoed from inside the house.

Now Luke looked even more confused.

"My brother's turtle," Meg explained. "He lost it, and I guess now he found it. But it must be dead."

Will suddenly appeared at Meg's side at the door. "I found Double-O-Seven under the couch," he said sadly, indicating his pet. Noticing Luke, he added, "I'm Will. My turtle's dead."

"That's too bad," Luke said sympathetically. "Do you want to have a funeral?"

"For a turtle?" Will said.

"Yes, for Double-O-Seven. I could play the James Bond song," he offered.

"Would you do that? Give him a funeral? With a song?" Will asked, amazed.

"Absolutely," Luke promised.

Watching Luke with her younger brother, Meg could hardly deny that her feelings for Luke were changing. Sure, he was a bit too self-satisfied, a bit condescending, and a bit of a deliberate loner—but all of the stuff that Roxanne had said about him was true, too. He was smart. And funny. And different from the other guys she knew.

Not to mention, Luke was pretty cute.

But he was going out with Roxanne now. Wasn't he?

* * *

Once the game ended, Meg rushed to the Vinyl Crocodile to see Roxanne. She supposed it wasn't very nice, crashing her friend's date with Luke, but she couldn't help herself. She just had to see what was going on with the two of them. Sprinting down the sidewalk she was surprised to find Roxanne standing outside the record store . . . alone.

"Why are you out here?" Meg asked, out of breath.

"Meg, whatever are you doing here?" Roxanne asked with exaggerated surprise.

"You're supposed to be with Luke—," Meg said.

Roxanne smiled mischievously. "No, I'm not," she said. "You are."

"What's that supposed to mean?" Meg asked, confused.

"Figure it out. I'll wait. I've got all night. I don't have a date or anything. Although, it's a little cold, so I hope you figure it out sooner rather than later . . ." Roxanne said, hugging her jacket more tightly to her body.

"Figure out what? And what do you mean you don't have a . . ." Realization slowly dawned over Meg. "You never liked Luke."

"No. I like East Catholic jocks and college boys on buses—"

"And he doesn't like you?" Meg interrupted.

"Nope," Roxanne said.

"You faked the whole thing so I would . . ." Meg's eyes were wide with shock.

"Meg, if you don't stop pretending you hate Luke, you're never going to notice how much you like him," Roxanne chided. Pointing inside, she added, "He's closing up."

As Meg started inside, Roxanne pulled her back.

"Wait a minute," she commanded. "Give me the clarinet. And the hat."

Dutifully, Meg handed both over.

And knocked on the door to the Vinyl Crocodile.

Looking for Luke.

Seven

"**O**ur next song is called 'You Really Got Me,'" Dick Clark announced. "It's sung by a group named The Kinks."

Meg watched as the *Bandstand* dancers exploded with movement. For once, Meg wasn't down on the floor dancing with them. She was sitting in a special seat, ready to appear on a new *Bandstand* feature called "Rate-A-Record." Once the song was over, Dick would ask her on national TV for her opinion.

Roxanne danced over, grinning. "You're doing great," she assured Meg.

"You think so?"

"Oh, yeah. So what are you gonna give this song?" she asked, which she herself was obviously enjoying.

"I don't know. I'm not really crazy about it. Maybe a seventy-five," Meg said cautiously.

"Be more positive," Roxanne said. "Michael Brooks loves positive. Give it an eighty-eight." With that piece of advice, she danced off.

The song ended, and Dick made his way over to the panelists. He pointed the mic in Meg's direction. "And our third panelist, Meg Pryor from East Catholic. Meg, what did you think of the song?"

"Well, I really liked it, Mr. Clark," she enthused. "It's got a good beat and you can dance to it. I give it—" She glanced at Roxanne, who stood off-camera giving her the thumbs-up. "I give it an eighty-eight."

Roxanne nodded her satisfaction, and Meg breathed a sigh of relief as Dick tallied up the final scores for all of the songs.

Roxanne was still complimenting Meg about her skills as commentator when they burst through the door to the Pryor house that afternoon. "First, a *Bandstand* regular, now a music critic," she exclaimed.

"Meg, we saw you on the show," Helen said as the girls walked in. Patty and Luke were seated at the piano.

"Luke watched Meg on *Bandstand*?" Roxanne echoed, intrigued.

"It was on the TV, but I was working on Patty's lesson," Luke said.

Meg turned and started up the stairs to her bedroom, Roxanne on her heels. "Come on," she said, trying to sound enthusiastic. "I have a new 45 I want to play for you. Bobby Vinton. I just got it yesterday."

"This next song is by a guy named Bach," Luke said loudly to Patty, turning back to the lesson. "While most people like the melody, I like it because it's got a nice beat and I can dance to it. I give it an eighty-eight."

Halfway up the staircase, Meg froze, a smile on her face.

When the piano music that had been playing steadily in the background stopped, the girls flew down the stairs to the foyer just as Helen was paying Luke for the lesson. Meg smoothed her hair and tried her best to look casual.

"Oh, Mrs. Pryor . . . there you are!" Roxanne vamped. "I've been meaning to ask you if you could show me how you fold those napkins so adorably. Like little boats or hats or something."

Helen smiled knowingly. "Yes, I know how much you love napkins, Roxanne," she said, leading Roxanne into the kitchen.

Now that she and Luke were alone, though, Meg was suddenly shy. "Patty's recital piece is really coming along," she managed.

"One appearance on Pick-A-Disk and you're a musical expert?" Luke teased, packing up some sheet music.

"Rate-A-Record. And no, I just know when I like something."

"So you're saying you might appreciate good music, too?" Luke challenged.

"If this is about Bob Dylan again . . . ," Meg began.

"Bob Dylan happens to be a genius. But this is about you," Luke said.

"Me?" Meg asked.

"Yes you, Betty. You can even bring Veronica if you like."

"Her name's Roxanne," Meg said, trying to sound annoyed. "And bring her where?"

Luke handed a piece of paper to Meg. "Somewhere we *play* music, not rate it."

The soaring, soulful harmony of a gospel choir greeted Meg and Roxanne when they finally made their way safely to their destination. The girls tentatively walked into the building listed on the paper Luke had given to Meg to find an all-black gospel choir rehearsing.

"In case you're still wondering," Roxanne whispered in her ear, "it's *definitely* not a date."

Meg spotted Luke accompanying the choir at a piano perched in the front of the sanctuary. "Rox, c'mon," she nudged her friend.

If Meg had thought that Luke was talented when she heard him play with Patty, now she was blown away. She slid into one of the front pews with Roxanne, unable to take her eyes off of him. He crackled with energy, wailing on the piano, keeping stride with the powerful vocals. Meg was out of her element, she knew . . . but she loved it. She felt she could watch Luke all night long.

After he had finished his piece, the choir began to pack up for the night. Roxanne casually wandered off, allowing Meg the chance to talk with Luke.

"Just wait until Saturday night. In the church, better acoustics. Packed house. That's when you really want to be here," Luke said. It was clear he really enjoyed this.

"How did you learn to play like that?" Meg asked, in awe. "It's—"

"Meg," Luke interrupted. "In case you missed it, that was an invitation."

Meg *had* missed it. She paused awkwardly, stunned.

"Meg? You think Roxanne would mind?" Luke asked.

"Mind what?" she replied.

"Not coming with you," Luke said.

A smile broke out across Meg's face.

This was most *definitely* going to be a date.

The next morning, Meg was up early. She decided to take advantage of having some time to herself and went to the den to sort through the family Christmas ornaments. She knew her mother was looking for a piece from her nativity scene that was missing, and she was hoping to find it.

The back door opened and Meg looked up to see JJ silently making his way inside. When he saw Meg he reacted, startled. "Oh, hey, Meg. I didn't think— you're up early," he offered, sheepish.

"Unpacking ornaments. You, too." She smiled at him. "Something tells me there's a really good story here."

"Listen," JJ said. "If Mom or Dad asks, you didn't see me." He crossed to the kitchen, poured himself some milk, and disappeared up to his room.

"But I was in *church*," Meg protested weakly, her father standing over her, seething. She should have known her trip to North Philly was bound to be discovered. "Patty," she grumbled under her breath. "That little fink."

"No, not Patty," her father said, glaring down at her and practically breathing fire. "Henry. Which means that for three hours on a Thursday night, nobody but Henry knew where you were."

Meg looked away. Her father had a point.

"What if something had happened to you?" her mother asked in a slightly softer tone.

"I was with Roxanne."

"And what if something had happened to Roxanne?" her father boomed.

"She was with me," Meg tried lamely. "I don't blame you for being angry. So I promise—after tomorrow night, I'll never go to that church again."

"I'll make it simpler," her father shot back. "You will *never* go to that church again. Including tomorrow night. You're grounded."

Tears sprung to Meg's eyes. "What? I can't believe it. I get grounded for going to church and JJ spends the whole night out and no one says a word." Flustered and upset, she fled the room.

Meg hadn't meant to get JJ in trouble, but she was sick of how overprotective her father was with her, while letting JJ slide. As the day wore on, she realized the ramifications of ratting out JJ.

After dinner she visited him in his room. "JJ?" she asked, stepping into his bedroom nervously. "Let me explain."

Turning away from his mirror, JJ looked at her before she could launch into her explanation. "It's a violation. Of a code," he argued, worked up. "Which says 'You don't rat out your brother.'"

Meg felt terrible. "I know. I'm sorry. I mean, how mad did he get? Dad?"

"This isn't about Dad," JJ argued. "I gotta go."

"Wait a second!" Meg said, angry. "Dad didn't ground you? That is *such* a double standard." She couldn't believe this was happening. Meg followed JJ out into the hallway, frustrated. Her mother stood at the top of the stairs. "It's not fair," Meg complained.

"I know," her mother agreed.

But there was nothing to be done.

The next evening Meg sat outside, perched on the hood of her father's car, gazing at the calm night sky. It was nice to be out of the house, away from the usual din, where she could gather her thoughts. She felt terrible about missing Luke's concert. She wondered how he was going to take it.

"So you got grounded."

Meg turned to see Luke standing in her parents' driveway.

"Your brother told me. He stopped by the concert last night. Told me all about it," Luke explained.

Meg smiled to herself, appreciating JJ's gesture to right things between them.

Luke pointed to the space next to Meg on the front bumper. "So, is this seat taken?" he asked.

"No, no," Meg assured him. He crossed to her and sat down next to her. The air was charged. Suddenly Meg was acutely aware of Luke's proximity. She liked having him close, but she wasn't sure how close they were supposed to be. Or what she was supposed to say. In the end, she decided not to say anything.

"Beautiful night," Luke said.

"Yeah," Meg agreed. She wasn't thinking about the sky, though.

"So what would you give it?" he asked.

Meg smiled, catching on. "I'd say probably somewhere between a seventy—"

"A seventy?" Luke asked, sounding disappointed.

"And a ninety-five," she finished. "Definitely closer to a ninety-five."

Luke wasn't looking at her, but Meg could still make out the traces of a smile on his face. She herself was beaming.

Without turning to face her, Luke took her hand in his. And in moments, innocently, the evening went from a ninety-five to off the charts.

Eight

Meg arrived at the WFIL studio late and found Rox talking to Michael Brooks. "Sorry I'm late. What are we doing?" she asked, as she slipped off her coat.

"We've got a Christmas show to rehearse," Michael announced, rushing off to organize the show. He started arranging the regular couples into two lines on the stage. He put the boys on one side and girls on the other, with Meg and Jimmy bringing up the rear of their lines. "You're there *before* the music ends, guys. Then it fades out and the ballad comes up— Tim and Shelly go right, David and Katharine go left, Meg and Jimmy go center. You all stop under the mistletoe and each couple kisses, and—"

"What?" Meg asked, cutting Michael off abruptly.

"Meg?" Michael prompted, sounding as though he thought she was crazy.

"What do you mean . . . kiss?" she asked.

"I think it's self-explanatory, Meg," Jimmy interjected.

"Jimmy, didn't you tell her?" Michael asked.

"Tell me what?" Meg asked, growing increasingly worried.

"The big Christmas kiss under the mistletoe. The viewers voted for their favorite couples and you three won," Michael explained.

"We did?" Meg asked. This was news to her.

"Are you okay with this, Meg?" Michael asked, suddenly serious. "You don't have to do anything you're not—"

"Meg, it's kind of a big deal," Jimmy cut in. "Kissing under the mistletoe in front of the whole country. It's an honor."

It wasn't that Meg didn't agree. She did think kissing on *Bandstand* was sort of a big deal.

That was the whole problem.

That afternoon, Meg came home from *Bandstand* to find her mother on the phone. "I think we should let him do it in his own time," Helen was saying.

"Whose own time?" Meg asked.

"JJ got a letter from Notre Dame!" Patty called from the living room.

"Really?" Meg asked, excited, looking to her mother for confirmation. Helen nodded.

Suddenly Will's voice could be heard from

upstairs. "All right!" he yelled. "Yeah, JJ!"

Realizing that JJ had gotten into school, Meg jumped into the air and threw her arms around her mother. "He got in!" she squealed.

"Did you hear?" Helen said into the phone. "He got in, Jack!"

Patty raced into the hallway and she and Meg jumped up and down, while Luke accompanied them on the piano with the Notre Dame fight song.

Later, as Patty and Luke were finishing their lesson, Meg came in to listen for a bit. She loved to hear Luke play. "I love that song," she said, as Patty mangled the final notes to "Calendar Girl" by Neil Sedaka.

"Thanks," Luke said. "Patty, practice the first six months and next week we'll do spring and summer."

"Oh, who won Best Couples?" Patty said, almost as an afterthought, as she walked into the kitchen.

"How did you know about that?" Meg demanded, embarrassed. Now there was no keeping the kiss situation a secret from Luke.

"What's Best Couples?" Luke asked.

"It was in *Teenzine*," Patty explained. "You could write in and vote for the best couples on *Bandstand*. Who won?"

"Tim and Shelly and David and Katharine," Meg said quickly. She paused. "And me."

Patty's eyes widened. "You and Jimmy Riley?"

"Who's Jimmy Riley?" Luke asked, trying to keep up with the conversation.

"Last year the couples kissed," Patty said, remembering. "Are you gonna kiss? You and Jimmy Riley?"

"I repeat, who's Jimmy Riley," Luke asked again.

"That's Meg's dance partner on *Bandstand*. They went on a date. But Meg gave him a black eye," Patty said. "So are you gonna kiss him?"

The doorbell rang and Patty rushed to answer it, leaving Meg to stare lamely at a rather displeased Luke. Roxanne pushed her way past Patty into the living room, carrying a box of ornaments. She immediately sensed the tension between Luke and Meg. "Problem?" she asked.

Meg glanced at Roxanne wearily, then grabbed Luke and dragged him into her mother's sewing room.

"What is your *problem*?" she hissed, once they were alone.

"You don't think for yourself. That's my problem," Luke spat. "Whoever they tell you to dance with, you dance with. Whoever they tell you to kiss, you kiss."

"What do you want me to do?" Meg implored. Couldn't he see that she really didn't have a choice?

"Well, for one, don't just *accept* everything without asking why. *Question* things. That's what I do."

"I question things," Meg retorted hotly. "You're not the only one who questions. You're not the *only* questioner."

"What are you saying?" Luke asked, serious.

"That I question." That much, Meg had thought, was obvious.

"So you're *not* gonna kiss him?"

"I *have* to kiss him," Meg insisted, feeling sick. This was bad. If she couldn't make Luke see her side of things, Christmas Eve would be ruined.

"You don't have to. You're choosing to," Luke corrected.

"Do you really think I want my first kiss to be on television?" Meg exploded.

Luke stared at her. "It's your first kiss?" he asked quietly.

"No," Meg said. "Yes."

"And you're gonna let them tell you who it should be? It's like you're their puppet."

Meg took Luke's words like a slap across the face. "Maybe I *want* to kiss him," she said, seething. "Did you ever think of that?"

She could tell her words had achieved the desired effect. Luke looked stunned. "I guess not," he said quietly.

Then he stood up and left.

The next day, Meg stopped by the Vinyl Crocodile on her way to *Bandstand* to try and sort things out with Luke. But he made it clear that she was going to have to make up her own mind about whether or not to kiss Jimmy on camera; he wasn't going to tell her what to do one way or the other. Meg respected his position, but she still didn't know what to do about the situation.

As she sat in the stands at WFIL deep in thought, Jimmy Riley sat beside her and asked, "You okay, Meg?"

"Sure," she said dejectedly. "Fine. I'm definitely . . . fine."

"You're so quiet today," Jimmy protested.

"I guess I have a lot on my mind," Meg admitted, sighing.

"Like what we're about to do?" Jimmy asked.

"Yeah," Meg agreed. "I just feel like everything's so fake. Fake snow, fake tree, fake kiss . . ." She trailed off.

Jimmy looked at Meg. "Maybe it isn't," he said earnestly. "Fake."

"What do you mean?" Meg asked, confused.

Just then, Dick Clark announced, "It's time for our special Christmas Couples Dance here on *American Bandstand*."

Meg wasn't feeling so well. Her heart was pounding and her throat was dry. Jimmy gently took her hand and led her to their marks on the dance floor. She glanced nervously around the studio, searching desperately for a way out.

After the other two couples had paused in front of the mistletoe and kissed with the audience applauding wildly, Jimmy stepped forward and extended his hand to Meg. She hesitated, listening to the echoes of the applause, and then stepped forward under the mistletoe.

This is it, Meg thought to herself. *I'm doing it.*

Jimmy leaned in and pressed his lips against Meg's, kissing her softly.

The sensation was entirely new for Meg. And yet, she instinctively knew exactly what to do. Meg's first kiss unfolded without a hitch—except for one thing.

She was kissing the wrong boy.

After the show, Meg stayed behind for a few moments, sitting in the bleachers and gathering her thoughts. Jimmy sat next to her, watching her, but she wasn't paying him any attention. She was staring straight ahead, thinking hard.

"Meg?" Jimmy asked, breaking her reverie.

"Yeah?" she replied.

"Whoever he is . . . the guy you were thinking about while you were kissing me—tell him you have a mean left hook," he said, smiling at her affectionately.

Meg smiled back and said good night, still thinking about how she was going to make things right with Luke.

Christmas dinner was homey and warm, as always, but the Pryors weren't in the spirit. Patty was angry at Will for accidentally ruining her gingerbread house, and Meg was cranky about her situation with Luke. Will was sad about upsetting Patty, and JJ was worried about being able to afford Notre Dame; he'd been accepted, but he hadn't gotten the scholarship that he was hoping for. Roxanne was disappointed about not being able to spend Christmas with her mother. And they had just heard the news that JJ's friend's older brother, Patrick O'Connor, was missing in action in Vietnam.

So it was with little enthusiasm that the group trudged off to Midnight Mass that evening.

"Jack?" Helen said questioningly. The group all turned to see what she wanted.

She pelted Jack with a snowball.

Everyone's tension dissolved instantly as they each scooped up handfuls of snow and bombarded each other, laughing. Meg found that she suddenly remembered what Christmas was all about. Her step felt about ten times lighter as she dusted herself off and scooted into the family car.

The snow continued to drift gently down as the Pryors approached the church. Their friends the O'Connors were waiting outside. Meg's father and mother rushed up to them with JJ, offering condolences and embracing them sadly. Meg, overwhelmed with emotion, hung back, tears streaming silently down her face.

She didn't know if she and Luke were going to make up, but she did know that her entire family was safe and sound and surrounding her. At that moment, she felt luckier than she'd ever been in her life.

"I heard, you know, about Patrick."

Meg started at the sound of Luke's voice. He had come up behind her while she was crying and she hadn't heard him approach. He folded her into his arms and wiped at a stray tear as she rested her head on his shoulder.

"I saw you on TV," he said, but it wasn't an accusation.

"I'm so sorry," Meg said. And she was. For everything. For hurting Luke, for squandering a first kiss on someone other than the boy she cared for.

"It doesn't matter," Luke said quietly.

The final church bell tolled, signaling that Mass was ready to begin. But before Meg could pull away, Luke cupped her face in his hands. He brushed her hair back and leaned toward her. And when his lips touched her own, Meg knew that she had finally had her very first kiss.

It was a very merry Christmas, at last.

Nine

"The Dave Clark Five?" Luke asked with derision, eyeing Meg's purchase questioningly.

"They're going to be as big as the Beatles," Meg assured him. "And you wouldn't like them. They're British."

"I wouldn't?" Luke asked, holding up a record of his own. "The Rolling Stones. British."

Meg made a face as he passed the 45 to her. "I'm not sure I'd like them. My brother says—"

"Three minutes and eleven seconds to find out if your brother's right," Luke said.

Meg dutifully accepted the record and walked off to the listening booths. Both were occupied, however; two girls stood inside of one, while Sam was in the other. Meg paused, feeling awkward, but Sam caught her eye and motioned her inside.

"Hi, Sam," said Meg, approaching him. "What are you listening to?"

"Paul and Paula. 'Hey, Paula,'" he told her,

holding out a pair of headphones. "Anita thought I'd like it."

Meg listened and then said, "It's good. I'd buy that one."

"I'm saving up, too," Sam explained.

"So . . . is Anita your girlfriend?" Meg asked.

"Kind of," Sam said noncommittally.

"Luke gave me this record to try. He thinks I need to learn about music."

"Nah," Sam said. "You dance on *Bandstand*."

Meg smiled. It was nice to feel that *someone* understood her. They listened to the Rolling Stones together. After a few moments of Mick Jagger's rugged wailing, Sam took off his headphones. "I don't think they're as good as the Beatles," he decided.

"JJ loves them," Meg said. "I can never decide which one to buy, and then I come in here to listen and I always want more than one. But they're so expensive."

"Yeah, I know what you mean," Sam agreed.

"So which one are you buying?" she asked.

"I think the Manfred Mann. You like 'Do Wa Diddy Diddy'?" Sam asked.

"I almost bought that too," she said. A lightbulb went off somewhere in Meg's mind. "We should trade. With each other. You probably have lots of stuff I don't and I have stuff you don't—and Luke probably has ten times what we have combined. Maybe he'd do it too."

Through the windows of the listening booth they could both see Luke tapping his fingers to whatever music he had playing through the store's main system. When Meg cracked the door to the listening booth, she and Sam could hear the strains of an obscure jazzy number. She looked at Sam and shut the door, realizing that a trading club with Luke probably wouldn't work. "Thelonius Monk," she said, making a face.

"Bob Dylan," Sam agreed. They both laughed.

"We can meet here tomorrow. After *Bandstand*," Meg suggested. There was no reason they shouldn't still have a trading club of their own.

"Okay," Sam said.

Finished with their planning, they both grew silent. Was this awkward, Meg wondered? The vague intimacy of their plan? She didn't understand why it would be wrong to meet with Sam after school—it was only music, after all—but somehow, she felt slightly uncomfortable. And judging from Sam's silence, he did too. But neither of them suggested canceling.

* * *

"How did it go with Michael Brooks?" Meg asked as she and Roxanne took their places in the *Bandstand* bleachers the next afternoon. Roxanne was campaigning to be named *Bandstand*'s new columnist for *Seventeen* magazine. But the competition was stiff.

"I think I made some headway, but I need to think of something really great," Rox replied.

As the show wound down, Michael Brooks took the stage to address the dancers. "Can I have your attention?" he called.

"Anyone interested in trying out for the position of 'Backstage on *Bandstand*' columnist for *Seventeen* can submit a writing sample to me and I will pass it along to the magazine for consideration. Have them on my desk by Monday afternoon. And please, no more gifts," he begged, before returning to the control booth now filled with homemade cookies.

"I can't believe this," Roxanne grumbled to Meg. "We have to work for it!"

Meg went straight from *Bandstand* to the Vinyl Crocodile, as she had promised Sam. The two of them set up camp by the register, fanning their 45s across the counter like a deck of cards. "And Bobby Vee and Jan & Dean and the Shirelles—,"

Meg said, offering a verbal catalog of her goods.

"I have the Shirelles," Sam said, flipping his record over. "The B-side's good."

"Oh!" Meg said, seeing a record that especially interested her. "You've got 'Nitty Gritty.'"

Finished with a customer, Luke swooped in to see what they were up to. "Interesting," he commented. "Most people *leave* with records. You come *in* with them."

"Just a few, Luke. I mean, we're still gonna *buy* records. It's not like we think this is a library."

"It's all right, isn't it?" Sam asked.

"Keep it in the listening booth so Mr. Greenwood doesn't see you," Luke suggested amiably. As Sam headed into the booth, Luke winked at Meg mischievously. She laughed, blew him a kiss, and went to join Sam.

Meg had such a good time listening to music with Sam that she didn't realize how late it was getting. She was surprised when there was a knock at the window and JJ was standing outside glaring at her. She couldn't imagine what he was so angry about. Sam left the booth and JJ stepped inside.

"What are you doing?" he demanded as soon as the door had shut behind him.

"Listening to music," Meg replied.

"You know what I mean, Meg. What are you doing with *Sam*?" he said pointedly.

Meg was slightly alarmed by JJ's tone. True, she had felt a bit uncomfortable yesterday when she and Sam had been making plans. But the truth was, she *liked* Sam and didn't think anyone could tell them not to be friends just because he was colored. Least of all her brother. "We're just trading records," she insisted.

"Why are you doing this?" JJ asked, exasperated.

"I don't know what you're talking about," Meg answered.

"Don't give me that, Meg," he said. "You know better. And you know how Dad feels."

"Dad isn't here," Meg said.

"Meg, I'm just trying to help you out," JJ said.

Meg could hear the concern in his voice, and she understood that deep down, this rebuke came from a place of love. But she knew Sam could hear their argument, and it pained her. "If you're trying to help me, then butt out," she said hotly.

"Just remember what happened. With you and Sam. And that cop."

Remember? How could she forget? She felt guilty about it every time she looked at Sam. But she was tired of people telling them that they couldn't be friends. Meg pushed past JJ into the store, wanting to make sure Sam was okay. But the front door was swinging shut.

Sam was already gone.

Meg stood nervously outside the door to Sam's apartment. She still hadn't talked to him since JJ had caused the scene at the record store. She thought Sam was upset and she wanted to set things right. But part of her wondered if by pushing, she was just making things worse. Finally Meg decided it was better to try than not to try, and with that, she knocked on his door.

The door opened, but Sam didn't look pleased to see her. "What are you doing here?" he asked.

"It's okay, isn't it?" Meg asked uncertainly. "You left these at the store the other day. And you didn't take any of mine." She held out a bag of his records, which he had left behind.

Sam glanced up and down the hallway, as if making a decision. "Come in," he said.

Meg hesitated. Going inside felt even more wrong than coming over had felt, though she couldn't put her finger on why. But she had to do it, she knew. At this point, refusing would be worse.

"How'd you know where I live?" Sam asked, getting right to the point. They both hovered near the front door.

"I looked in the phone book. And I know you take the number eight bus, so . . ."

"So what do you want?" Sam asked.

"I came to return your records," she said. It didn't sound right, even to her ears. She started again, "What JJ said—"

"I didn't hear what he said," Sam cut her off abruptly.

"He was wrong," she continued. "I know you're mad, and you have every right to be. But I just wanted to say . . . I don't feel the way he does."

There. It was out. All of her feelings, on the table. She knew that a friendship with Sam would be risky for both of them—but to her it was worthwhile. The question was, did he feel the same way?

Sam hesitated, looking as though he didn't know what to say. Finally, he managed, "I wasn't mad."

"You weren't?" Meg asked skeptically. "Then why'd you leave like that?"

"I just didn't want to cause any more trouble for you," he said.

"It's not fair," she said simply, hoping he would understand what she meant.

Sam nodded shortly. "Just the way things are."

"I guess," she said. She knew that for Sam, unfairness was a way of life, more than she'd ever know. While this was her first experience with racism, it was something he dealt with every day. It wasn't fair. But she didn't know how to make it better.

"I got the new one by Herman's Hermits," she offered.

Sam allowed himself a small smile. "'I'm into Something Good.'"

"Yeah," she said, steeling herself. "I'll be at the Vinyl Crocodile tomorrow. After *Bandstand*. Are you going to be there?"

Sam didn't say anything, and Meg wondered if coming here had been the right idea after all. Then he said, "I don't know."

Crestfallen, she returned home.

The next day, after *Bandstand*, Meg headed off to the Vinyl Crocodile as she did nearly every afternoon. She stood in the booth listening to "You Are So Wonderful" by Marvin Gaye. She liked the song a lot, but she had too much on her mind to really enjoy it.

Luke slid the door to the booth open. "I'm going to have to lock up soon," he told her.

"I know," she said. He looked at her sympathetically. He scanned the store to be sure no one was watching and stole a quick kiss. It was nice, but it didn't make her problem go away. When Luke stepped out of the booth, he moved aside to reveal that someone else had just come into the store.

Sam. With a stack of 45s in his arms.

Sam approached the listening booth with a bit of apprehension. Meg removed her headphones and opened the door, waving him in eagerly.

"Wasn't sure you'd be here," he said.

She smiled at him. "I wasn't sure *you'd* be here," she said. But he was, and that was all that mattered. She wished she could tell him that his friendship was important to her, that his friendship made her question some of the people closest to her. But it was too much to say. It was almost too much for her to understand. For now, they'd just listen to their music.

Together.

Ten

Valentine's Day. The mere mention óf the holiday brought to mind bouquets of flowers, boxes of chocolate, and cards bearing sentimental greetings.

Unless, of course, one happened to be dating the Bob Dylan of her generation.

Well, maybe "Bob Dylan" was an exaggeration, Meg allowed, but as Luke idolized the folk singer, he had also adopted some of Dylan's cynical ways.

Which, much to Meg's dismay, somehow extended to Valentine's Day.

The two were discussing the upcoming East Catholic Valentine's Day dance while Luke filed records. Filed records, and offered pitiable reasons the dance was off-limits.

"'Do You Love Me,' 'Baby Love,' 'Chapel of Love,' 'Love Me Do,'" he recited mechanically as he filed. "Those are the reasons we can't go to the dance."

"We can't go because of some really good love songs?" Meg asked, not following at all.

"And because we'd have to hear each and every one of them in a row Saturday night. On a pathetic record player. In the gym. Why would we want to do that?"

"Because it would be a fun thing to do with your girlfriend on Valentine's Day?" Meg offered, knowing somehow that that wasn't going to be the winning argument. Sure enough, Luke looked at her and shook his head, more in disbelief than anything else. "You don't believe in Valentine's Day?" Meg asked, refusing to comprehend.

"I believe," Luke said, offering Meg a short glimmer of hope. "I believe it's a holiday created by card companies and flower shops to keep up their sales." Reading Meg's look of disappointment, he continued, "Meg, we don't need somebody telling us when or how to be romantic." He leaned in and gave her the kind of kiss that told her exactly how he felt. The kind of kiss that *almost* made Meg feel better.

Almost, but not quite. "Oh, and the chocolate companies," he added as an afterthought, pulling back. "They're part of the conspiracy too."

"Okay, I'll admit it," Roxanne confessed dramatically. "I'm starting to worry. Nobody's asked me." She was, of course, referring to the Valentine's Day dance. To which Meg most likely wasn't going either.

"What about Bobby Mahar?" Meg asked. "I thought you thought he was thinking about asking you."

"He's probably still thinking about it," Rox reasoned. Then, as if struck by a random thought, she asked, "Did I suddenly become repulsive?"

"No! Of course not," Meg assured her.

"I'll tell you one thing," Rox said. "I don't care who I go with, I am not missing this dance. It's our first one as *Bandstand* regulars. Right?"

Meg bit her lip. "Um . . . I don't think we're going, me and Luke," she said quietly, bracing herself for Roxanne's reaction.

"So he's *not* taking you to the dance, *not* getting you flowers, *or* cards, *or* chocolate?" Roxanne asked, aghast. "And that's okay with you?"

Meg nodded. Her expression was all the answer Roxanne needed.

"Are you going to talk to him?" Roxanne asked.

"Right after the show," Meg replied. There was no reason to pretend to her boyfriend that things weren't important to her, if they were.

She just hoped he'd understand.

When Meg arrived at the Vinyl Crocodile, the line of customers at the register extended to the back wall of the store, but she didn't let that stop her. She marched right up to the front. "Luke," she said with determination, "I like flowers, and chocolate, and Valentines. And most of all I like to dance. So even though *you* think it's a made-up holiday, I'm going to the East Catholic dance, and I think it would be really great if you came too." Bravado faltering, she added, "Is that okay?"

"That's okay," Luke agreed, smiling.

"It is?"

"It is," he repeated.

"Good," she said, beaming. "I mean, great."

"Mom, can I have an ant farm?" Will asked that night at dinner.

"No, you may certainly not," Jack replied. "We're still finding JJ's damn ants in our closet."

"Roxanne," Helen said, smoothly redirecting the converstion, "how are you getting to the dance?"

"I think my date's got his license," Roxanne said.

"Bobby asked you?" Meg asked.

"Not yet," Roxanne admitted.

"Sarah Mahar says her older brother didn't ask you 'cause you have a reputation," Patty said.

"That's enough of that," Jack said sternly.

"I'm sure he didn't mean it that way," Meg rushed in, seeing Roxanne's stricken look.

"I think he did," Patty said, grim.

Roxanne sat quietly, not saying a word.

Roxanne wasn't any chattier the next afternoon as she and Meg studied in the East Catholic library. "Okay, what is Northern Rhodesia now called?" Meg quizzed.

"Who cares?" Roxanne said glumly.

"People who live in Northern Rhodesia. And people who have a test on Monday," Meg said gently. "It's Zambia."

"That'll come in handy next time I'm in Africa," Roxanne muttered.

"Stop worrying about it," Meg said sympathetically.

"You spend your whole life thinking boys *like* a girl with a reputation, and then you find out no one'll ever ask you to a stupid dance," Roxanne complained.

"Not no one," Meg reminded her. She pointed over at Warren, a classmate of theirs who had already invited Roxanne to the dance. Roxanne, still holding out for Bobby, had turned him down. "He's a nice guy," she said encouragingly.

"Maybe," Roxanne said thoughtfully.

"No, he *is*," Meg insisted. She liked Warren. He was planning to enter the priesthood.

"Maybe I *should* go with him. He's going to be a priest. The perfect antidote to a reputation."

Meg nodded, understanding Rox's logic. "Because nobody's going to be whispering about what *you* two did at the dance."

"Exactly. Me and Father Warren." Roxanne stood, her mind made up. She winked at her friend. "I'll be right back."

The next evening, Meg stood in front of the bathroom mirror putting the finishing touches on her hair. Luke was due to arrive any minute, and she wanted to look perfect. One look at her and he'd change his mind about Valentine's Day. She clasped her grandmother's locket around her neck and stepped back, satisfied with her reflection.

The doorbell rang, and Meg went downstairs to greet Luke.

When she got there, however, her father had beaten her to it. "I want you two back by ten," he was telling Luke sternly.

Will stood behind him, emulating his father's authority. "You heard him," he repeated solemnly.

"Yes sir," Luke said to them both.

"We can wait for Roxanne and Warren in the living room," Meg told Luke, leading the way.

"You look very nice," Luke complimented her as they took a seat in the living room.

"Thank you," Meg replied, scrutinizing Luke as subtly as possible for any hint of a hidden corsage, and finding none. She sat back against the couch, suppressing a sigh.

"So," Luke said mockingly, "how do you think they decorated the gym? Giant paper hearts or red-and-white crepe paper streamers?"

"Giant paper hearts," Meg said resignedly. "I was on the decorating committee."

Meg, Luke, Roxanne, and Warren stood outside the gym along with a few other students waiting to have their pictures taken before they went into the dance. Meg couldn't help but notice the lavish corsage Warren had brought for Roxanne. "It's really pretty," she told him, pointing to Roxanne's wrist.

"Thanks, my mom picked it out," he said.

The doors to the gym opened as a stray dancer emerged, and the hallway was momentarily filled with a swell of music.

"'Book of Love,'" Luke commented dryly. "What a surprise."

"Come on, Warren," Roxanne said, leading her date away by the arm. "I want everyone to see us together." They marched off, leaving Meg and Luke alone together.

"Don't you want to go in and dance?" Meg asked nervously.

"I'm not really the dancing type," Luke said.

"Really? I mean, you really don't like to dance?" Meg asked. She couldn't believe that *anyone* really didn't like to dance. "I guess I didn't know that."

"The music I like isn't the kind you dance to," Luke explained.

His words hit Meg hard. She knew that she and Luke didn't have a whole lot in common, but she had assumed that theirs was a case of opposites attracting. Suddenly, however, she found herself wondering if their differences would ultimately come between them. What a realization to have on Valentine's Day.

Fortunately, Meg was saved from further reflection when Sam walked into the school with a date on his arm. He smiled at Meg. She could tell he was happy to see a familiar face.

"Hello, Sam," Luke said. "You get dragged into this thing too?"

"Not really," Sam said, seeming much happier to be there than Luke was. "Luke, Meg, this is Anita. We used to go to school together. At Washington."

"Sam talks about you all the time," Meg said to Anita.

Anita shot Sam a look that said, *All the time?*

"Well, not all the time," Sam quipped, laughing.

"Better be all the time," Anita told him. "Nice to meet you Meg, Luke."

"Next song—," Luke guessed, "either 'Baby Love,' or 'My Boyfriend's Back.'"

Meg took in Anita's dress, which was lovely. Her gaze lingered on Anita's corsage, as well. "That corsage is beautiful," she told Anita.

"Thank you," Anita said. She flashed a grin at Sam. "I told you everyone would notice."

From inside the gym, 'Baby Love' broke out. "It's a gift," Luke bragged, oblivious to the conversation.

"You wanna go dance?" Sam asked Anita. She nodded, and the two of them headed off into the gym. Meg glanced at Luke.

The two of them stood alone in the hallway.

Again.

The evening was a disaster. All night, Meg and Luke had stood awkwardly side by side, while he joked about the clichéd music, the tacky decorations, and the corniness of Valentine's Day in general. She had thought that Luke might find it worthwhile to like something because he knew it was important to her—but apparently, that was not the case.

Meg headed off down the hallway to find Roxanne. "Rox!" she said, surprised to have found her friend so quickly.

Roxanne spun around. "Meg, do you and Luke wanna come to the music room? The surprisingly frisky Warren and I are gonna drink a few of these." From behind her back, she pulled a six-pack of beer that Meg assumed was from the janitor's closet.

"I need to talk to you," Meg said urgently. "About Luke."

"Follow me," she ordered. They went to the music room, where Warren waited.

"I think I have to break up with him," Meg said, once they were sitting down again.

"What?" Roxanne asked.

"How come?" Warren chimed in.

"We're really different," Meg explained, feeling confused and miserable. "We don't like any of the same things. And if we're not fighting, we don't really have anything to say."

Roxanne nodded, looking as though she didn't really see the problem. "Uh-huh. But you like kissing him. And you think he's cute. Which he is," she said.

"Rox . . . he made me feel bad about liking

Valentine's Day. Why do I want a boyfriend who makes me feel bad?" She thought back to a conversation she'd had with JJ, when he told her that she shouldn't be with anybody who didn't want to be with her. Now, more than ever, she knew what she had to do.

Meg found Luke standing outside of the school's front entrance, looking at the stars. "Sorry," he said, when she approached him. "I didn't mean to disappear."

"That's okay. You didn't want to be here," Meg said matter-of-factly.

"But you did," Luke said quietly. "Let's go someplace else," he suggested, taking her hand and leading her back inside the building.

Once inside, they found their way into an empty history classroom. Luke began uncertainly, "Either I'm dragging you someplace you don't want to be or you're dragging me someplace I don't want to be, and the rest of the time we fight about it."

"That's not true," Meg said, even though she knew it was.

"I like you too much to keep doing this," Luke said.

"Are you . . . breaking up with me?" Meg asked.

She knew it had to happen, but this moment was so much more painful than she could have imagined.

"I think so," Luke said. "I don't want to. But I think I am."

"Luke—," Meg said, then stopped. True, she'd planned to break up with him. But somehow, the fact that he'd gotten there first changed the playing field. Her instinct was to argue, to dissuade him. Even though she knew he was right.

"I'll walk you home," Luke said, curtailing further discussion.

"That's okay," Meg said. She didn't think she could handle the long walk home. "I'll go home with Roxanne. Really. It's okay."

"Bye, Meg," Luke said, leaning in for a last, lingering kiss.

"Good-bye, Luke," Meg said sadly. She watched him walk away, thinking, *Happy Valentine's Day.*

Eleven

"**H**e thinks I can't be serious," Meg complained, pretending to play "Roll Over, Beethoven," during band practice, while surreptitiously filling Roxanne in on the latest news of her relationship with Luke.

"You can't go from making out to just being friends," said Roxanne. "That's tampering with the laws of basic human nature."

"Except, we could never work as a couple, Luke and me. He thinks that just because I dance on *Bandstand* I can't be serious. I can be *very* serious," she said, setting her expression to one of solemn dignity.

Roxanne looked at Meg doubtfully. The band hat stood atop Meg's head in stark contrast to her dignified pose. "I believe you," she said nonetheless. "But it's never gonna work."

"We can be friends, 'cause we have something different: ground rules. No more treating at the movies, no free advance copies of records, no calls after eight at night—because eight to ten, that's boy-friend time—and no making out." She folded her arms dramatically for effect.

Roxanne looked horrified. "No making out?" she echoed.

"Miss Bojarski! Either pick up a trombone or leave the field!" Father Crane called out, irritated at having his band practice disrupted.

Roxanne plucked a trombone from the arms of a very surprised passing student. "Thanks, Mark," she said, smiling.

Laughing, Meg and Roxanne continued with "practice."

That afternoon, Meg was late to *Bandstand*. She whizzed in just as the dancers were taking their places. "You just made it," Roxanne said, as Meg slid into the bleachers.

"Congrats, Roxanne," a camera guy said, as he walked past the girls. "When're you gonna write about me?"

"Why's he congratulating—oh my gosh! Your *Seventeen* column! I completely forgot!" Meg exclaimed. Roxanne had won the competition, and her first column had just been printed. "Rox, I'm sorry. I've been so preoccupied with Luke and everything . . ."

"Well, you better read it. You're in it," Roxanne informed her.

After dinner, Meg and Roxanne retreated to Meg's room so that they could go over Roxanne's column. Meg flopped onto her bed and eagerly flipped the magazine open to the right page. She scanned down the first few paragraphs . . . then stopped dead. She glanced up at Roxanne, and then back down to the page, not believing what she was reading. "'*Bandstand* sweetheart Meg Pryor, otherwise known as Jimmy Riley's better half . . .'" She glared at Roxanne accusingly.

"Meg, I don't know why you're so upset," Roxanne protested, confused.

"'. . . has accomplished her life's goal by becoming a regular on *American Bandstand*. Who needs history and math when you're a bubbly blonde who can look *that* cute doing the Mashed Potato?'" Disgusted, she tossed the magazine aside. "That's what you really think of me?" she asked, hurt beyond belief. When Luke had told her she wasn't serious enough, she'd been insulted. But to hear Roxanne suggest the very same thing felt like the ultimate betrayal. "Thanks a lot, Roxanne," she said.

Thanks for nothing.

* * *

The next day, as Meg got off the bus, she caught sight of Sam. She was really glad to see him—not only because it had been awhile, but also because spending time with him would take her mind off what Roxanne had written about her. "Sam, wait!" she called, running to catch up with him.

"Hi," he said, once she was walking alongside him. "How was *Bandstand*?"

"We saw Bobby Rydell. 'Make Me Forget,'" she said. "Sometimes I can't believe I get to see all these people. Someday you've gotta come."

Sam paused reflectively. "Maybe someday," he agreed. Meg knew it wouldn't be as easy as she was making it sound.

"What happened at track?" she asked, changing the subject.

"I got to race Grady. You were probably rooting for JJ," Sam said.

"I was kinda hoping for a tie," Meg said diplomatically. "Are you going to celebrate or something?"

Sam nodded. "Sort of. I'm meeting Luke."

"Luke? Really?" Meg asked, trying not to appear overly interested. "Where're you going?"

"To the Pantry. Just for a burger," Sam said. "You wanna come?"

Meg glanced at her watch. She had time, and technically, this wasn't breaking any of her new rules. "Are you sure that would be okay?" she asked.

"Yeah, why not?" Sam said.

"Right, why not," Meg agreed.

We're all just friends.

The Pantry was a typical diner, bustling with customers. Little Richard's "Good Golly Miss Molly" blared from a corner jukebox as waitresses raced around delivering heaping plates of food. Sam and Meg stood at the front of the restaurant, by the hostesses' stand, waiting to be seated.

The hostess approached the stand. She didn't appear to see Meg and Sam, however. She looked right over their shoulders at a couple standing behind them. "Just two?" she asked the other people.

"I think we were first," Meg cut in.

"Go ahead and take that table in the back," the hostess said to the couple, pointing toward a vacancy.

"We'd like a table, if there's room," Meg said. Something was going on here—*that* was for sure.

The hostess looked from Meg to Sam. "I'm sorry, there's not," she said.

Meg scanned the restaurant quickly. "But there's one right there—" she said, pointing to the nearest table.

"Let's just go," Sam said uneasily. "It's okay."

Meg switched tactics, aiming to reason with the hostess. "We just want a burger. We're waiting for our friend . . ."

The hostess was now ignoring Meg, ringing up another customer's bill.

"It's fine, Meg," Sam insisted. "We'll wait for Luke in the parking lot. We can go somewhere else." He didn't sound upset or angry, just resigned.

He led her outside, where the two of them stood in the cold waiting for Luke. After a moment, Meg rushed back into the diner and came face-to-face with the hostess. "You can't treat people that way," she said.

"Actually, I can," the hostess argued. "This is my restaurant. I own it . . . and I don't have to serve you and your boyfriend."

Meg's mouth dropped open in an *O* of surprise. "He's not my boyfriend, but even if he was, he's a person. With feelings," she said hotly. "And he's my friend."

The next day when Luke arrived for Patty's lesson, it was Meg who let him in.

"Hi," he said shyly. "You look really pretty."

"You sure compliments aren't breaking the ground rules?" she teased. He shrugged. She glanced up the stairs and said, "I'll go get her."

"Meg," he said, before she could dash off. "That was brave, what you did at the diner. Standing up to that lady . . . that was a brave thing to do."

When she'd come out of the diner last night she had seen Luke in the parking lot with Sam. They'd gone to eat elsewhere, and hadn't had any further discussion of the hostess.

"I just wanted to have a burger with my friends," Meg said simply. It was the truth. "Sam. And you."

With that, she ran up the stairs to get Patty.

The next day, Nina Simone's record was playing over the speakers at the Vinyl Crocodile. Meg had stopped by to swap records with Sam, but was mesmerized by Nina's voice until Luke wandered over to say hello.

"Hi," Meg said. "I came to meet Sam to trade records." She looked at her watch. Sam was late. "But maybe he's not coming."

"I could tell him you were here," Luke offered.

"Thanks," Meg said.

Luke handed her a record. "What's this for?" she

asked. Records were, after all, against the "ground rules."

Luke smiled. "Old time's sake. It's Donovan, Britain's answer to Dylan," he explained. "It's an advance copy. *Catch the Wind.*"

Dylan, Meg thought. *Some things never change.*

Then again, did she really want them to? Her thoughts were so confused these days, and her friendships were growing increasingly complicated. Maybe a little stability was a good thing. "Thanks," she said to Luke, meaning it.

Meg couldn't push Sam if he wasn't ready to spend time with her, she knew, and her friendship with Luke would develop naturally over time. But she was desperate to patch things up with Roxanne. They hardly ever argued, and when they did, it was practically impossible to stay mad at each other.

Thankfully, Roxanne felt the same way. The next day she read Meg a glowing column she had written about Meg's many virtues.

"Roxanne," Meg said, "I appreciate you writing all these nice things about me, but you really don't have to give this to *Seventeen.*"

"I know," Roxanne said, her eyes twinkling. "I wasn't planning to. That was just to get you to stop being mad at me. Even if *Seventeen* isn't gonna publish this, you know what I think of you. Right?"

Meg smiled. She knew. She knew a lot of things. Most of which she had only recently started to realize. Friendships, for instance. She knew friendships could be difficult. They required understanding, compromise, and patience. But the right friendships were worth everything.

Twelve

"Make a wish," Michael Brooks said.

In the background, "Hippy Hippy Shake" played throughout the *Bandstand* studio. It was Roxanne's birthday, and Meg and Michael had conspired to throw her a party on the set.

"Okay, let me think," Roxanne said, squeezing her eyes shut.

"Roxanne, sweetheart, make a wish," Michael urged, putting his face close to her own and speaking softly.

Roxanne opened her eyes, smiled at Michael, and blew out her candle.

Meg could tell exactly what her wish was from Roxanne's lovestruck expression. Never mind that just that afternoon during gym, they had sworn off boys forever. Meg was beginning to wonder if her good friend had sworn off *boys* with the intention of pursuing *men* instead.

* * *

"Did you hear what he said?" Roxanne whispered excitedly once the girls had taken their seats in the bleachers. "He said, 'sweetheart.'"

Meg's spirits sunk. She'd been afraid that Roxanne was developing a crush on Michael—one that couldn't lead anywhere good. "Yeah, he *said* it," Meg agreed, trying to infuse the word with meaning, "but I don't know if he meant it."

Roxanne studied Meg as if she were crazy. "He said it," she said simply. "And Meg, have you ever smelled him? He wears Old Spice," she said dreamily.

Oh no, Meg thought. *She's got it bad.* She tried the logical approach. "Roxanne, I know Michael's really cool and nice, but he's older than us, you know," she pointed out as gently as possible.

"It happens," Roxanne countered. "There was an article about it in *Look* magazine. It's called a 'May-December' romance."

"I just don't want you to get your hopes up," Meg said.

But she suspected it was way too late for that.

When Roxanne had first spoken to Meg about her crush on Michael Brooks, Meg knew her friend was in deep. But at dinner, when Roxanne used her second birthday wish on Michael, Meg knew they'd hit a point of no return.

"Of *course* I wished for Michael Brooks," Roxanne exclaimed impatiently, once they were back in Meg's bedroom doing homework. "Number one, he called me 'sweetheart.' That's also number two—*sweetheart!*" she repeated, dancing around the room. "Number three is the little cake from *Bandstand*—I wonder if he baked it himself."

"Stop wondering," Meg said. Then, turning back to her homework, "I've got a question: When *did* they build the Panama Canal?"

"I've got a better question: Who cares? Stop doing your homework," Roxanne said suddenly, dropping to her knees in a pleading stance. "Meg, you have to do me a favor. You have to go to Michael for me—"

"No," Meg said. She was already in this deep enough.

"Meg! Ordinarily I'd handle this myself, but—"

"No," Meg repeated firmly.

"I promise, whatever you find out, I'll live with that," Roxanne swore. "If the answer's no—"

"No!" Meg insisted.

No. No. No.

* * *

Somehow, all of those "no's" had evolved into a resigned "yes" over the course of an evening of begging. The next day, Meg approached Michael. She felt awkward and more than a little bit silly.

He was on the phone, but waved her into his office.

She stood in the doorway, nervous. "Okay," she began. "I have this friend, who has a crush on you. She, uh, dances here, with us, on the show," Meg stammered.

"Your *friend* does?" Michael asked skeptically.

"Uh-huh. And I said I would ask if it was even a little bit possible that you and her—my friend—"

"Whoa, whoa, wait," Michael said, stopping her midstream. "First of all, it's a nice thing, so you don't have to pretend it's a 'friend.'"

Oh, gosh! He thinks I'm lying to cover up my own crush! Meg realized with horror. "No! It is! It actually is a real live friend!" she protested, a bit hysterically.

"Of course it is," Michael agreed, in a tone that suggested he was basically placating her. He leveled her with a more serious look. "Meg, I'm a guy with a lot of rules," he explained. "Like, no dating girls at work. Also there's an age difference. Don't know if you noticed."

Meg hung her head. "Uh, yeah, we noticed," she said.

"But the main thing is this: I'm involved with somebody. Not sayin' I'm engaged. Not yet, but . . ." He looked at her.

She nodded to show she understood. Inside, she felt a bit of relief. It would be easier to tell Rox he had a girlfriend than that he just wasn't interested.

Satisfied that the issue was resolved, Meg leaned closer to the monitor to see what Michael was working on. It was footage of Shirley Ellis singing "The Nitty Gritty." She remembered when that had aired. "Why are you looking at this?"

"Dick wants to do a 'Memory Lane' show," Michael explained. "A greatest-hits special kinda thing."

"Oh, my gosh! That would be so much fun, to go through all those old acts!" Meg said. It sounded like a dream job to her.

"Yeah, I guess it is. Hey—you've watched the show for a long time, right?" Picking up a small phone, he said, "Don, gimme the Frankie Valli song again, will ya?" He turned back to Meg. "Look at this," he said, indicating a clip cuing up on the monitor. "You can give me your opinion."

And just like that, Meg and Michael were working together.

* * *

Meg felt guilty. She hadn't called Rox when she had gotten home from WFIL the night before, and she'd been steering clear of her all morning at school—no easy feat. She just couldn't stand to be the bearer of bad news on the subject of Michael.

"Meg! Didn't you hear me?" Roxanne called, rushing to catch up with her in the crowded hallway.

"Uh . . . no," Meg lied. "Sorry."

"Didn't call me last night," Roxanne singsonged.

"I know," Meg said, biting her lip.

"And I'm dying to know what Michael said," Roxanne pressed.

There was no more putting off this moment. "Roxanne, he said there's no hope," she said, as a hurt expression crossed Roxanne's face. "Rox," Meg said, backpedaling slightly to soften the blow, "he has a girlfriend. He told me. A serious girlfriend. You're not mad at me for telling you, are you? Because you said if the answer was no . . ."

Roxanne nodded, looking glum. "No means no," she agreed quietly.

But Meg had a feeling the situation was more complicated than that.

* * *

At *Bandstand* that afternoon, Meg saved Roxanne her usual spot in the bleachers. But Roxanne was sitting somewhere else. Meg approached her tentatively. "Why are you sitting all the way over here?" she asked. "You said you weren't mad about me telling you what Michael said."

"That was before I heard," Roxanne snapped. "Vicky Maglio told me she saw you in the booth with Michael for a whole hour after *Bandstand*."

Oh, no, Meg thought desperately. How was she going to explain to Roxanne about this? "It's not what you think," she said quickly. "He's doing this 'Memory Lane' show for Mr. Clark and I was helping him, and Rox—" It was difficult for Meg to keep the excitement out of her voice even though she was trying to be sensitive. "He actually wanted my *opinion* of what groups, and you know, what songs . . ."

"Sounds like fun," Roxanne said flatly.

"More than that. It was—I even thought of some things he didn't. Rox, it was something I could do. Me. I mean, I love dancing on the show, but *this* . . . I don't know if you understand." She wasn't sure *she* fully understood it just yet. But it had something to do with passion and talent and being able to do something meaningful.

"I understand," Roxanne said, surprising Meg. "I understand that you want Michael all for yourself."

Thirteen

"**Y**ou are such a phony!" Roxanne exclaimed. "Pretending you're not interested in Michael . . ."

Days had passed since Meg had spoken to her about Michael. She hadn't made much headway in convincing Roxanne she was working with Michael in a strictly professional capacity. The whole thing was starting to drive Meg a little bit crazy. Today at *Bandstand*, it was all Roxanne talked about—that is, when she was even talking to Meg. "I'm not interested in Michael," she repeated for what had to be the bazillionth time. "We're working on that—"

"Yeah, yeah, I've heard it before. The 'Memory Lane' special," Roxanne said, unimpressed.

"This is ridiculous," Meg said, aiming for a logical tactic. "Roxanne, I'm not interested in Michael Brooks. And if I were, which I'm not, I wouldn't do anything about it anyway, because if I were, which I'm not, *you are*, which is crazy—and not just normal crazy; it's crazy crazy—but you are so—I would never do that." Meg took a deep breath.

"I believe you," Roxanne said shortly.

Meg thought perhaps she'd misheard her friend. "You do?"

Roxanne nodded. "I guess the only question now is, how can I use *your* relationship to *my* advantage?"

Meg arrived home a few minutes later than usual and found her family, minus JJ, already seated for dinner. "Sorry I'm late," she said.

"Call next time, please," her mother admonished.

"All right, I just have to say this," she said eagerly. "Something amazing happened to me today."

"Let me guess—it's about dancing on *Bandstand*," Patty said sarcastically, making a sour face.

"No, it's about *working* on *Bandstand*," Meg corrected, refusing to let her enthusiasm be tamped. "Michael Brooks asked me to help him with a special show they're doing."

"That's wonderful, hon," her mother said.

"What show?" Will asked, demonstrating slightly more interest than Patty.

"They're picking the best performances from the history of *Bandstand* and putting them all in the same show."

"Sounds like a rerun, if you ask me," Jack grumbled.

Meg was floored. Someone was asking her opinion about a television show that the whole country would watch, and her father had just dismissed it, the way he did everything else that was important to her.

"Mom, I'll need you to help me type up a list of songs after dinner. Please," she said.

"They paying you for this? The big shot producers?" her father grilled her.

"No," Meg admitted. Couldn't he see that the experience itself was payment enough?

"So they've got you working for free," he commented.

"It's an opportunity," Meg protested. "To learn how they make television."

"I've seen that show . . . couldn't be that hard. 'You—dance.' 'You—sing,'" he mocked.

Helen interrupted. "Some people go their whole lives trying to find something they love. And Meg's already found it."

Meg was touched. It was nice to know her mother, at least, understood her.

Just then, JJ walked in. He had fractured his leg in a recent game, and was now in a cast. Meg felt bad for him; she knew he hated being sidelined. Notre Dame hadn't offered him financial aid, so he was now banking on a football scholarship from Lehigh.

"Oh, JJ. Tomorrow morning. The cemetery. You, me, and Pete," said Jack.

Every year since Jack's father had died, Jack, JJ, and Jack's brother Pete went to visit his grave on his father's birthday. It was a tradition for the men in the family. When Will was old enough, he'd join them.

"Yeah, I know," JJ said, rising abruptly from the table.

"Can I fix you a plate, hon?" his mother asked.

"Nah, I'm not hungry. Just gonna go rest my leg," he said, heading off to his room.

Later that evening, after Meg and her mother had finished typing up the song list, Meg went to the kitchen for a glass of milk. JJ was telling Jack he should probably stay home from the cemetery and stay off of his leg. Which apparently meant that *Meg* would have to go in his place.

"If you can't come, I'll just take Meg," Jack said, as though Meg weren't even standing in the room.

"I told you, there's a special meeting tomorrow at *Bandstand*," she cut in.

"And if we're back in time, you'll be there," her father said, unrelenting.

"Dad, Michael Brooks asked me specially," she begged.

"Meg, this is what families do. It's not a punishment," her father said.

But that's what it felt like to Meg.

Meg called Roxanne that night to commiserate. "I mean, is it me?" she moaned. "Or is he being a hundred percent unfair?"

"A hundred and eight percent," Roxanne agreed.

"I need you to give Michael my list," Meg said, knowing Roxanne would relish the task.

"But I thought you said you'd be back in time for *Bandstand*?" Rox asked.

"Maybe. My dad said he can't promise," Meg said glumly.

Meg could hear Roxanne's squeal of excitement over the telephone line. "Think about it. Just me and Michael alone in the booth . . ." She paused, lost in her own private reverie. "There *are* love songs on your list, right?"

Meg began to read off her song titles so Roxanne could write them down and take them to Michael.

It wasn't the same as being there, but it would have to do.

* * *

The cemetery visit took longer than expected—the Pryors spent at least two hours tending to the gravesite, which was overrun with weeds. Still, Meg would have made it to the show if it hadn't been for the early dinner at a greasy spoon called Dutch's that her father and Pete insisted upon going to every year. The three of them sat in a vinyl booth in the run-down diner.

"There's no way I can make it back now," Meg said, chin in hands.

"Maybe next time," her father said, unsympathetic.

"There is no next time," she responded. "I'm going to miss my meeting. And Michael will never trust me with anything again."

"Nothing's more important than what we did today," her father asserted.

"Maybe to you," Meg said, meaning it.

"Your family comes before some TV show," Jack said decisively. He rose from the table. "I'm gonna wash up," he said. "Order me a drink and the pie."

"That's your dad," Pete said, trying to sound cheerful. "Family comes first."

"'Cause it's important to *him*. He never cares

what's important to anyone else," Meg insisted.

"Someone's gotta keep up the traditions," Pete said. "That's why he stops here. The pie's terrible, but Pop loved this place. That's why he made you come today. He wants to make sure you'll do it. When *he's* gone."

Meg could see the truth in what Pete was saying. She just wished her father would try to understand her point of view, since she was trying to understand his.

Meg was thrilled that Michael had chosen almost all of her suggestions for the "Memory Lane" special. When she arrived at WFIL the next day, he gave her a thumbs-up in the hallway. "Good work. On your list," he said.

Proud to have contributed something to the show, she danced with even more than her usual abandon. When "Catch Us If You Can" by the Dave Clark Five was played, Meg and Roxanne practically took over the dance floor. As Meg was dancing, she happened to glance off into the wings. What she saw nearly took her breath away.

Her father.

Standing. Watching her.

Meg was flooded with joy. Her father would

never be a fan of *Bandstand* the way he was of, say, football. But he was there. He was taking an interest in something that was important to her.

And that was the most important thing of all.

Fourteen

April brought with it bright skies, sunshine, warmer temperatures, and a new fashion craze: the miniskirt. "Meg—will you look at the skirt on Ashley Bowen?" Roxanne said, mouth agape, as the two danced past Ashley's high hemline.

"Her parents went to London and bought her practically a whole new wardrobe," Meg said, repeating the latest gossip.

"How'd she get away with that?" Roxanne asked, her voice tinged with longing.

"She goes to Lincoln," Meg said.

Both girls glanced at each other. Simultaneously they said, "Public school."

Roxanne sighed wistfully. "That proves it. God is not merciful. Because if He were, these legs would not be stuck at East Catholic," she said mournfully, looking down at her own woefully long skirt.

As the show wound down, Roxanne headed off to quiz Ashley on her new clothes. Meg was packing up her belongings in the dressing area when Michael Brooks approached her. "Meg, I need for you and Jimmy Riley to promote the *Bandstand Medley* record by signing some autographs. It was supposed to be David and Katharine—"

"But Katharine has the mumps," Meg finished. "I heard."

This was exciting! The *Bandstand* team had decided to produce a record collection of the top performances on the show. Traveling around and especially signing autographs sounded like a ton of fun!

"German measles," Michael amended. "Which is why I need *Bandstand's other* favorite couple to step in. It's at three o'clock at a store called the Vinyl Crocodile."

Meg's face fell. "The what?" she asked.

If Meg was worried about how Luke would take the news, she didn't have to wait long to find out. She came home to find him finishing up Patty's piano lesson.

"So, I'm glad I ran into you," Luke said, turning to Meg once Patty was gone. "I heard about the *Bandstand Medley* signing and I wondered if there's anything special I need to know about Donald and Katharine."

"Well, for starters, he likes to be called David, because that's his name. And actually, Katharine's got the German measles . . . so I'm going to take her place. Actually, me and—"

"Mr. Mistletoe," Luke surmised.

Meg nodded. "Do you think it'll be weird? Since you're my ex-boyfriend and Jimmy's my fake boyfriend," she said.

"Ex . . . and fake," Luke repeated, making it clear that she had nothing to worry about. "You want to know what I think is weird? That anyone would buy the *Bandstand Medley* record. *That's* weird."

Flash! Just when Meg's eyes had adjusted to the light, another camera went off, temporarily blinding her again. The Vinyl Crocodile was a madhouse, teeming with teenage fans of the show—and of Meg and Jimmy!

They sat side-by-side at a table signing copies of the record. The crowd loved them! "We can ask questions, right?" one eager boy asked.

"You just did," Jimmy teased. Meg shot him a scolding look, and the two exchanged the type of glance usually reserved for "real" couples. They had a great rapport. Just like when they danced— chemistry.

"Since you two are such a neat couple—"

"Only the best couple on the show!" Jimmy interjected.

"Yeah," the fan agreed heartily. "I wanted to ask you, what do you think makes you so good together?"

Meg thought about the question for a moment, glancing in Luke's direction. He also seemed pretty interested in what she had to say. She replied, "Well, it's definitely nice to be attracted to someone, but I think it's also important that you have stuff in common. Things you like to do—" She faltered when she saw Luke turn away abruptly.

"Music and movies and dances, and, well, Meg and I like all the same things," Jimmy finished, saving her. "Plus, she happens to be the most talented, smartest, sweetest girl on the show. I'm just the lucky guy on her arm."

The female fans waiting in line swooned collectively. Meg smiled at Jimmy. She had to admit, he could be awfully charming when he wanted to be.

"What's your favorite new band?" someone else wanted to know.

"The Animals," Meg and Jimmy said simultaneously, laughing. Their fans were thoroughly smitten.

* * *

"And what about the little girl? With the red hair?" Jimmy laughed.

"The one who pretends with her friend that they're Jimmy and Meg?" Meg was hysterical at the memory. The signing was over and it was time to leave the store.

"You were great, Meg," Jimmy said.

"No, you were the one," Meg protested. "Because I kept fumbling. Oh, how about when we both said the same thing at the same time. That was—"

"It's almost like it was real. Like we were a real couple," Jimmy said, his words echoing Meg's own thoughts.

"I even started to believe it myself," Meg confessed. "I mean, what we were saying." She flushed. She hadn't meant to actually admit that to Jimmy.

"Well, it's easy. At least for me. Because from my side it is real," Jimmy said, completely throwing Meg for a loop. "Maybe that means we oughta give it another shot, Meg Pryor from East Catholic."

Meg looked up at Jimmy, unsure of what to say. He seemed to read her hesitancy, and was understanding.

"Think about it," he said, giving her a quick kiss on the cheek. "I'll give you a call."

* * *

Meg did think about it. She thought about it for a long time, in fact. Even though she knew she still had feelings for Luke, there would always be a soft spot in her heart for Jimmy. And now that she and Luke were broken up, well—maybe Jimmy was right. Maybe it was time to give them another shot as a couple. So she decided to go out on another date with him.

"I'll be home after the movie!" she called to her mother, flying down the front stairs to meet Jimmy.

"Hi," Jimmy said, grinning his typical toothpaste smile. "You look sharp."

"Have a good time, Meg! You too, Jimmy," Patty shouted from the living room.

Meg turned to reply to her sister and immediately realized what Patty was up to—Luke stood next to her at the piano, ready to begin the lesson.

Meg was flooded with a mixture of emotions. Mostly she felt awkward, heading off on another date with Luke standing in the room, and a little sadness because she wasn't dating Luke anymore. But she also remembered how he had left the Vinyl Crocodile without saying good-bye the other day, and how he had, in fact, been the one to ultimately suggest that they break up. She knew that she wasn't doing anything wrong by going out with Jimmy. "Let's go," she said to Jimmy, and the two were out the door.

During the drive-in movie, Jimmy took great pains to make conversation with Meg, but she was completely distracted. Seeing Luke on her way out the door had really thrown her off. But Jimmy was being so sweet that she tried hard to focus on him. When he drove her home, he kissed her good-bye. And this time, they kissed for real—not just for *Bandstand*. But when he drove off, Meg didn't go inside.

There was someone else she had to see.

The Vinyl Crocodile was dark by the time Meg arrived. Luke stood on a ladder against the front window, hanging a poster, a lock of hair hanging in his eyes. He looked surprised when he saw Meg rapping on the door.

"I thought you were out with—," he began as she walked inside.

"I was. Don't say anything," Meg said.

"Excuse me?" Luke asked, confused.

Meg was confused, too. "Luke, don't say anything. Just . . ." Then, almost as though her body was acting independently of her mind, Meg reached out, pulled Luke toward her, and kissed him. It was different than it was with Jimmy Riley. More than different. And just as suddenly she pulled away again.

Luke looked at her, stunned.

"I'm sorry," she faltered. "I have to go."

She turned and ran from the store.

"Big deal," Roxanne said. "So you kissed two boys in one night. Okay, so you like kissing boys. So do I."

Meg was frustrated. Kissing Jimmy and Luke one after the other had stirred up all sorts of emotions, but instead of helping her figure them out, Roxanne was basically suggesting that Meg should kiss as many boys as she wanted whenever the spirit moved her! "No, see, I *had* to, Rox. See, when Jimmy kissed me it was sorta . . . 'He's So Fine,' you know, like the song? Fun, and *fine*, and . . . and so I had to try to remember what Luke sounded like— *kissed* like—and . . ."

"And?" Roxanne prompted. Meg's story was much more interesting than her sewing project.

"Well, he was a little more . . . 'Going out of My Head,'" Meg finished. She hoped that by putting it in the context of music, Roxanne would understand what she was feeling.

"Like, 'Day and Night, Night and Day—and Night, Going out of Your Head'? Like that? *Really*? Well, then," Roxanne said thoughtfully. "You've got to do something about that."

The Vinyl Crocodile was closed, there were no customers around to bother them, and Meg had to get this off of her chest. ". . . and we're always arguing, and a lot of the time I don't even like you, and Jimmy Riley is sweet and nice and says all the right things and—"

"Meg—," Luke tried again.

"Luke, just listen for once," Meg insisted. "All we ever do is fight. And whenever I think we ran out of things to argue about, we find more. And so we broke up, but since then, as hard as I've tried, I can't stop thinking about you. About you and me." Feeling vulnerable, she finished her rehearsed speech. "Okay, you can talk now."

"Me, too," Luke said.

"You too what?" Meg asked, feeling irritable. She had just laid her heart on the line, and he wasn't making any sense.

"All of it," Luke said.

Meg suddenly remembered something. "Wait—darn it. I wanted to do that whole speech after I did this."

She stepped forward and placed a 45 on the turntable, cranking the volume up to a respectable level. "Going out of My Head" by Little Anthony & the Imperials.

Luke cocked his head and listened to the music for a beat or two. Then he looked at her. *Really* looked at her. Like he was taking in her face, which he knew so well, all over again. Then he kissed her.

And all at once, Meg was. Completely. Out of her head.

Fifteen

Being on *Bandstand* had a number of perks, like dancing on national television with cute boys and meeting famous singers. But Meg was finding that being on the show wasn't bad for her social life at East Catholic, either. She and Roxanne were rushing down the school hallway, late to a meeting of the Prom Committee.

Inside the activity room, music blared from a portable radio. A small group of girls—all very cool and beautiful—were gathered around a banquet table. The table was covered with samples of decorations and mocked-up invitations, which the girls were now evaluating. Carol Bendiger, a senior with beauty-queen looks, held court.

Spotting Meg and Roxanne entering the room, she waved warmly. "Meg, Roxanne! Welcome to Prom Committee!" she said.

Meg glanced excitedly at Roxanne. This was it. The popular girls were inviting them into their circle. *We've officially arrived,* Meg thought.

"What do you need us to do?" Roxanne asked enthusiastically, immediately getting into the spirit of things.

"Here," Carol said, handing them a clipboard. "I've broken down everyone's tasks. You'll be responsible for decorating—with other attendants, of course—collecting money for the formal photos, taking coats and—oh, you'll need to wear white gloves with your prom dress."

Meg tried to hide the surprise she felt. A *dress*? She looked at Roxanne, who looked equally concerned. "We have to wear a prom dress?" Meg asked.

"Is that a problem?" Carol asked.

"Not a problem," they said simultaneously.

"You girls probably have closets full of great dresses, being on *Bandstand* and all," Carol said, sounding truly impressed.

How could they argue?

A few hours later, Meg and Roxanne were the only remaining committee members left standing. They picked at the remains of a pizza with Carol and Carol's best friend, Maureen, as they contemplated balloon color combinations.

"Oh, I nearly forgot!" Maureen said. "I'm getting the perfect picture for Senior Snaps."

"What is it?" Carol asked.

"I went to City Hall and got my picture taken on Mayor Tate's lap," Maureen said, giggling.

"That's so wicked!" Carol said gleefully.

"What's 'Senior Snaps'?" Meg asked.

"Everyone tries to get their picture taken in the most unusual place," Carol explained.

"Billy White got his taken on Edgar Allan Poe's grave. And Claire Montgomery snuck into Sister Mister's room and put on her habit," Maureen offered.

"Wicked!" Carol said again.

"You know what would be wickedest?" Roxanne asked. Looking uncertain, she tried again. "Most wicked? Getting your picture taken at *Bandstand*. Standing at Dick Clark's podium."

"What a great idea!" Maureen enthused.

"Could you do that? Really?" Carol asked, eyes shining.

"Oh, I don't think that Michael would—," Meg began. The idea made her very nervous.

"I'm sure we can arrange it," Roxanne said, cutting Meg off.

And with that, the decision was final.

That night, when the doorbell at the Pryor house rang, Meg told her mother she was headed out to a

Prom Committee meeting. *After all, it's not too far from the truth,* she rationalized.

Meg and Roxanne took the bus to WFIL—which was slightly creepier at this hour of the night. Rox had come by earlier to scope out the best way to sneak in, and now, she propelled herself through an open window on the first floor, reaching out to pull Meg through.

"I can't believe we broke in," Meg said, glancing nervously around the room. The place was dark and quiet—vastly different from the normal hubbub found at *Bandstand*. It was unsettling.

"The window was open, Meg. So technically we *snuck* in, not broke in."

Meg was not comforted. "Make sure to tell that to the police when they arrest us."

"Meg, we're not getting arrested. Carol will take her picture and we'll be gone in five minutes," Roxanne assured her. "They're gonna love us for this." Seeing that Meg still hadn't moved, she urged, "Quit being such a chicken. Go let Carol and Maureen in. I'll try to find the lights."

I'd better get this over with, Meg decided. She made her way slowly to the front door, her eyes eventually adjusting to the lack of light. Fortunately, she knew the studio like the back of her hand.

She reached the front door and pushed it open, expecting to find Carol and Maureen. But when the door opened, Meg bit her lip. Carol and Maureen had brought friends.

Twenty minutes later, the party was in full swing. One of the boys was playing at being a DJ, and music pumped through the studio speakers. Some of the seniors were drinking beer, and a few guys in one corner were swinging cameras across the floor. Everyone was dancing and enjoying themselves.

Except Meg.

"I should have brought my grandmother," Roxanne complained. "Seventy-two years old and she still would've been more fun than you."

"This was a big mistake," Meg said, eyeing the boys who wielded the cameras. Something was bound to be broken, or worse, destroyed. And then what?

"Some of the cutest boys at East Catholic are here. Meg, we are the coolest sophomores in history. C'mon, don't ruin it," Roxanne said, practically begging.

"The picture! Carol!" Maureen urged.

Carol took off her East Catholic sweater and tossed it into the bleachers. She smoothed her crisp, creaseless blouse and struck a pin-up girl pose behind Dick Clark's podium. Maureen aimed and snapped the photo. "This is a really good one, Carol," she said eagerly.

Carol grabbed the mic like an emcee. "And now I'd like to introduce our guest today. A wonderful friend, a girl of great talent, here to show you the latest dance steps . . . Meg Pryor!"

All of the revelers clapped and stamped their feet, cheering for Meg. Roxanne shoved her forward, into a particularly cute boy who was more than happy to catch her and drag her to the stage. Despite herself, Meg found she was enjoying the attention.

The DJ cued up Diana Ross and the Supremes.

What the heck? Meg thought. *If you can't beat 'em, join 'em.* She jumped on stage and began to lip synch and dance with Carol, who followed her step for step.

Meg and Roxanne were mouthing along to Smokey Robinson's 'Mickey's Monkey' in the *Bandstand* bleachers when Meg was struck with an attack of paranoia. "Did Michael Brooks look at you funny?" she asked Roxanne, slightly panicked.

"Like this?" Roxanne said, making a silly face. "Relax, he has no idea."

But as the show cut to a commercial, Michael stepped over to address the group. "I have some pretty serious news. Last night, someone broke into our stage," he said, his face grave. "Whoever it was had a party and did a hundred and twenty dollars' worth of damage to one of our cameras."

Meg felt terrible. She had no idea that equipment had been ruined!

"I'm pretty sure that whoever did that is sitting here today," Michael continued.

Meg felt sick. She was sure she and Roxanne were going to be found out.

"And I'm pretty sure that whoever did it is gonna get caught," Michael finished, meaning business. "And dealt with."

Meg thought long and hard about what to do. Roxanne thought that if they confessed, they would be kicked off *Bandstand*, and neither of them wanted that. But Meg felt terrible about the broken camera. She'd been saving money to buy a dress for the prom, but decided to donate her prom money to *Bandstand*, toward a new camera. She'd give the money anonymously so that she and Roxanne wouldn't be found out.

"I wish I could help you pay for a new dress," Carol said sympathetically, when Meg explained the predicament to her. She needed to tell to Carol why she wouldn't have a new dress for the prom.

"But I just bought my prom dress and shoes, and if I ask my parents for more money right now they'll get suspicious," Carol finished.

"Carol, I wasn't asking you for money," Meg said.

"I know, but I want to do something. I have a dress I only wore once—to my cousin's wedding. And it's really beautiful," Carol said. "It cost two hundred dollars. I got it at Gimbels in New York."

"You want to lend me that dress?" Meg asked, eyes wide with excitement.

"No, silly, I want to *give* it to you," Carol said.

Meg couldn't believe her luck. She felt like she had just won the lottery. Impulsively, she threw her arms around Carol.

Roxanne walked into the activities room to find Carol and Meg hugging and laughing. "What's going on?"

"Rox—Carol's giving me a really beautiful dress to wear to the prom!" Meg said.

For a moment, Meg thought she saw her friend falter, but then Roxanne's trademark grin was back, wide as ever. "That's great. Wow," she said.

If Roxanne was being anything but sincere, Meg didn't notice. She was too caught up in the moment.

Now, if she could only give Michael the money without giving herself away, everything would be perfect.

Meg was sitting in Michael Brooks's chair in the control room, lost in thought, when he walked in.

"You're a producer now, Meg?" he teased, seeing her in his seat.

"Oh, I'm sorry," Meg said, sitting up. Now that he was here, she was feeling nervous.

Meg had meant to leave the money anonymously, but when it came down to it, she knew that would be the wrong thing to do. Covering up the party would serve her, but it wasn't right. She owed Michael the truth. "Michael, I'm sorry," she said, handing him the envelope. Tears filled her eyes.

Michael peeked inside the envelope and handed her a handkerchief. "Here. And I'm not kicking you off of *Bandstand*."

It took a moment for his words to sink in. But when Meg realized what he had said, she couldn't help but cry. "You're not?"

Michael shook his head. "This, however, will be put toward the camera. And you're gonna pay me back for the whole thing—you and whoever else was involved. And if it ever happens again, Meg—you're gone. Consider yourself on probation."

Meg nodded vigorously.

"You know," Michael said casually, before she could slip out the door. "People are always leaving things here. You think maybe we should start a Lost and Found?"

Meg had no idea what he was talking about. "I guess," she said.

"In fact, I think I'll make that your job. Part of your rehabilitation," Michael said. He opened a drawer and pulled out a sweater, tossing it to Meg.

Meg grabbed at the sweater and looked it over. "East Catholic," she said, her cheeks coloring.

"I found it here the morning after the break-in."

It took a moment, but the implication hit Meg like a ton of bricks. "If you knew, why didn't you—"

"Because if I'd had to come get you, you would have been kicked off the show," Michael said plainly. He motioned her out of the control room.

Meg realized how lucky she'd been. She had a prom dress, some new friends, *and* a second chance at *Bandstand*. She wasn't going to blow it.

Sixteen

As prom drew nearer, Meg found herself spending more and more time with Carol. She was excited to have a new friend—and it seemed like Roxanne liked Carol, too.

After school, the three girls went back to Meg's house so she could try on Carol's dress. Sky-blue chiffon fell across her body. The dress was perfect, hugging her body in all the right places. "Thanks, Carol, for giving it to me. I've never had anything this beautiful," Meg said sincerely.

"Now if only we were *going* to the prom instead of working at it," Roxanne said, appreciating how lovely her friend looked all dressed up.

"Who's taking you? Your summer boyfriend?" Meg asked Carol.

Carol shook her head. "Steve? No. You know how summer boyfriends are—best kept in the summer. I'm going with a friend of my brother's."

Roxanne sighed wistfully. "Last summer, I fell in love eleven times. I hardly had time for a tan."

"Meg, can I use the phone to call my mother?" Carol asked.

"Sure, it's in the hall downstairs," Meg replied.

Carol left the room to make her call and Meg gazed in the mirror, playing with the hem on the dress.

"I like her," Roxanne said suddenly.

"You do?" Meg asked. That was good. It meant that they could all be friends.

"At first I thought she was kinda pushy. And you know how I hate pushy. But I have to admit, she's growing on me." She approached Meg and gathered Meg's blond curls into a bunch. "Maybe we should wear our hair up," she suggested, posing in the mirror. Meg smiled, happy that all of her friends could get along.

"Now, what do you have by way of shoes?" Carol asked, coming into the room.

"Oh! Shoes!" Meg had nearly forgotten about those. She disappeared into her closet and began to rummage. "I think I have a pair that might work," she said.

"I'm hungry," Roxanne decided. "I'm thinking root beer and potato chips. Anyone want anything from the fridge?"

Carol and Meg declined. Roxanne disappeared off to the kitchen.

Meg emerged from the closet triumphantly, waving a pair of open-toed heels. "What do you think of these?" she asked.

"Perfect," Carol said. "Oh, I nearly forgot—I'm having a sleepover tomorrow. So we can all do our nails and stuff for prom. Can you make it?"

"Wow, yeah. Thanks. Roxanne has this new nail color I was gonna borrow. 'Flamingo Pink.' I'll tell her to bring it."

"The thing is," Carol said carefully, "and this is not me—I don't feel this way at all—but some of the other girls . . ."

"What?" Meg asked, suspicious.

"They don't like Roxanne," Carol said. "And they don't want her there."

Meg felt guilty being invited to Carol's without Roxanne, but Carol was her new friend, and she didn't want to risk losing her. Plus, she kind of *wanted* to hang out and get ready with all of the popular senior girls. So when Roxanne asked Meg to sleep over the night before prom, Meg did something awful. She lied.

She told Roxanne she needed her beauty sleep—and then she went to Carol's.

She didn't regret her decision for long. Carol's

house was wonderful. Her bedroom was lavishly decorated and the girls were set for a night of primping. Most were in their nightgowns with their hair in rollers, some sitting underneath hair dryers. Meg filed her nails as Carol looked at Meg's latest letter from Jimmy Riley.

Jimmy had showed up late to *Bandstand* one afternoon and told Meg he had enlisted in the Marines. She was sad to be losing her dance partner and friend, and worried about him having to go off to war. But they had shared one last dance together in the silence of the empty studio, and she had promised to write to him. She thought back to the days before she'd met him—she never dreamed they'd become partners, much less friends.

"Where'd you say he was going again?" Carol asked, snapping her out of her reverie.

"Saigon, he thinks," Meg said. "It's in Vietnam. But he's in North Carolina now, in infantry training."

"I can't believe you kissed him on TV," a girl named Paula gushed. "What did your real boyfriend say?"

"Luke? He was mad. But not for long," Meg replied.

"Let's take out the Ouija board," Paula suggested.

"I want to find out who at school likes me the most."

"Speaking of people at school, Meg," Maureen jumped in, "don't take this the wrong way, but your friend Roxanne, she's a little . . ."

"Loud," Susan, another senior, added.

"You've got her all wrong," Meg protested. "I mean, I know she comes on a little strong at first—"

"A *little* strong?" Paula interjected.

"She's got a good heart and she's the best friend I—"

"Meg, you don't have to defend her," Carol said. "Didn't you bring some new 45s?"

"Yeah, I brought a bunch," Meg said, relieved to be rescued. "My friend Sam and I, we swap records so we can hear all the new—"

"Is he on *Bandstand* too?" Paula asked.

"No, he goes to East Catholic. Sam Walker," Meg said.

The girls froze. They recognized his name.

"That colored kid on the track team?" Maureen asked in shock. "I can't believe you're friends with him."

"That is so cool," Susan said, squirting whipped cream from a can straight into her mouth.

"Definitely. My parents would kill me if I were friends with a colored boy," Carol agreed. "What's he like?"

"He's really nice. And smart. And he likes the same kind of music I do. This one's his." She put Petula Clark's "Downtown" on the turntable and let it play. The girls seemed surprised by her style, but after a few minutes, they were lost in the music.

Meg danced to the record, thoughts of Roxanne and Sam banished completely. For now, at least, she was just having fun.

Meg was in trouble.

When she'd gotten home from Carol's the next morning, her mother told her Roxanne had called. Which meant Roxanne knew that Meg had lied to her. And now, they were at *Bandstand* and Roxanne wasn't speaking to Meg.

"Roxanne," Meg said, cornering her in the hallway before the taping began. "I know you know I was at Carol's."

"I can't believe you lied to me," Roxanne said, marching off to the bleachers, where the rest of the dancers were getting ready to take their places.

Meg followed fast on her heels. "I just . . . I thought it might hurt your feelings."

"You know what hurts, Meg? You lying to me. So Carol didn't invite me. Big deal. It's not like she was having a big party or something. Right?"

Meg hesitated. She felt horrible, adding one lie on top of another. But she didn't think she really had a choice. "No," she said, feeling miserable.

"If the two of you have a sleepover, you can tell me," Roxanne said.

"You're right, I should have," Meg said.

"I'm only mad because you lied. What'd you guys do?"

Meg thought quickly. "Nothing much. It was so last minute. She forgot she had shoes to match my dress, so . . ."

"Did she say anything about me?" Roxanne asked.

"Oh, uh . . . I don't think so."

"So she likes me, right?"

"Yeah . . . ," Meg said, feeling uncomfortable. "I'm sure she does." *Carol said it was the* other *girls who didn't like Roxanne, not her. So it's not a lie.*

"Good," Roxanne said brightly. "So next time we'll all sleep over together."

Meg winced inwardly. There was no way to tell Roxanne that Carol wasn't interested in one big sleepover.

Prom was magical, and Meg and Roxanne loved being dressed up, even though they had to work.

But at some point in the evening, the magic ended.

Meg wanted to talk to Carol about prom photos. But she was only about halfway down the hall when someone grabbed her arm.

"I just want to know why you lied. Twice," Roxanne demanded, hurt etched across her pretty features.

What could have happened? Meg wondered. *Did Roxanne overhear something?* "Rox, you don't understand—," she started.

"You're right," Roxanne snapped. "I don't. Explain it to me. Why did you say it was just you and Carol? Why did you lie about all those girls? About the party?"

Meg hated the thought of telling more lies, but she couldn't tell Roxanne that the other girls didn't like her. She just couldn't. "I . . . I don't know," she said.

"You know why. You lied because you didn't want me around. You want to be friends with Carol and her friends and you don't want me to," Roxanne said. "Because I'm not cool enough, or pretty enough . . . You want them all to yourself."

Oh no, Meg thought. "No, that's not it. Roxanne, I swear it's not."

"And the saddest thing is, you don't have the decency to admit it." Roxanne shook her head, steaming. "I don't even know what I'm doing here." She stalked off, leaving Meg alone.

Roxanne didn't come home with Meg after the prom. The next night, Meg went to the Bojarski apartment to try and make up with her friend. She found Roxanne on the rooftop, smoking a cigarette and listening to a small transistor radio.

"I'm sorry to bother you," Meg said softly. "Your mom said you were up here. Would you mind if I just sit up here for a while?"

Roxanne shrugged. "Free country," she said.

Meg sat tentatively in the chair next to Roxanne. After what felt like a long moment she said, "It's about trust. A person has to trust another person and not throw away their friendship because of what they think a person is doing when that's not at *all* what they're doing. At all."

Roxanne was quiet for a heartbeat. Then she said, "I know they don't like me." It was a statement of fact. "I'm not stupid. It took me a while, but—"

"It's only because they don't know you," Meg insisted.

"They know me enough not to want me at their slumber party," Roxanne said. "And I guess that bothers me a lot more than it bothers you."

"No, it does. It bothers me," Meg said.

"Don't worry about it, Meg. Things can't stay the same forever," Roxanne said, in a flat tone that worried Meg.

"What do you mean?" Meg asked.

Roxanne took a long drag on her cigarette. "People grow up. They change. Plans, too." She looked directly at Meg. "I'm not going down the shore with you this summer."

Meg's eyes flew open. "But you always go. Every year since we were five." She couldn't imagine a summer at the shore without Roxanne.

"Like I said, things change," Roxanne repeated. She looked down at the ground. "Maybe you should go."

Meg looked at Roxanne. There was nothing she could say or do that would make things better. And so, resigned, she rose and left her friend alone.

Seventeen

"**Y**ou can't stay mad forever, Roxanne. It's bad for your complexion." Meg and Roxanne were packing up from another afternoon at *Bandstand*. Meg was—unsuccessfully—trying to convince Roxanne they *needed* to make amends. *Bandstand* was holding a hop down in Wildwood, and Meg couldn't imagine going without Roxanne.

"I told you, I'm not mad. Besides, I have flawless skin," Roxanne replied.

"Which of you are going to be down in Wildwood? For the hop?" Michael polled, prompting an enthusiastic chorus from those who were going.

Meg raised her hand. "I'm going, but Roxanne—"

"Wouldn't miss it," Roxanne finished.

"Not for the world," Theresa McManus added, shooting a smug look at Meg.

Michael nodded, making notations on his clipboard.

As Michael left, Meg turned to Roxanne, confused. "But you . . ."

"I never said I wasn't going, Meg," Roxanne said. "I said I wasn't going with *you*." Then she drove the knife in deeper. She turned to Theresa and asked, "What time do we leave?"

Roxanne turned to leave, Meg following at her heels. "How can you drive down the shore with Theresa? You hate Theresa!" Meg said.

"I've been known to misjudge people," Roxanne replied.

"Look, I know I lied to you. I did one stupid thing. But Roxanne—we've been going down the shore since we were five. You and me."

By now the two had reached the bus stop at the corner. Someone called, "Meg!" and they turned to see Carol pull up in a gleaming new Ford T-Bird. The top was down and "Foolish Little Girl" by the Shirelles blasted from her radio.

"Wow, Carol! That car is so—," Meg said admiringly.

"Showy?" Roxanne whispered, strictly for Meg's benefit.

"Graduation present from the folks. You girls want a ride? Get out of the heat?" Carol offered.

Meg looked at Roxanne. It really was hot out. But accepting Carol's offer basically meant choosing Carol over Roxanne.

"You go ahead, Meg. I'm enjoying the sun. Good for my *complexion*," Roxanne said meaningfully.

Meg looked awkwardly at Carol. "Thanks, but I think we'll . . . stick it out," she said.

"Suit yourself. But I'll see you down the shore, right, Meg? We're doing the Crest Club the whole time."

"Sure," Meg said.

With one last wave, Carol sped off. Meg looked up to find Roxanne staring at her. "You and me? Since we were five? I guess we're not five anymore."

It was a triangle, and Meg didn't see any way out of it.

If anything could get Meg's mind off of her troubles with Roxanne, it was a vacation in Wildwood. The house her parents rented was small and homey. Meg felt relaxed the moment she stepped through the door. She changed into her bathing suit and a pretty sundress, tied her hair into a low ponytail, and headed off to the Crest Club. If Roxanne wasn't going to forgive her, she was going to have to find another way to enjoy herself.

The Crest Club was an upscale beach club. Uniformed cabana boys provided guests with chairs, towels, and matching umbrellas, and brought them fancy drinks on trays. Meg stood off to the side for a moment, taking in the scene and feeling slightly out of place. Then she spotted Carol talking to a pale, redheaded girl and two boys. One of the boys, she noticed, was very good-looking, with an athlete's build and an easy smile.

Meg approached the group uneasily, but when Carol saw her she immediately lit up. "Meg! You made it," she said warmly.

Meg smiled, settling in a seat next to Carol.

"This is Meg Pryor. A friend of mine. She—"

"You're a regular on *Bandstand*, I recognize you," the redhead said. "Did you meet the Beach Boys? I think I'm in love with Brian Wilson, though Mike's kinda cute, too, and—"

"Slow down, Holly," the cute boy told her. "She just got here."

"No, it's okay, I love the Beach Boys too," Meg assured them.

"Meg, this is Shane Waldon," Carol said, finishing up the introductions. "And I told you about Stephen. Stephen Patterson—Meg Pryor."

He extended his hand to Meg, grinning a dazzling smile. "Steve. It's nice to meet you."

"So, *Bandstand* is going to be having a hop down here," Holly said. "Ron Diamond's coming all the way from Philly to DJ."

"And the Kinks are going to be there," Meg said. She couldn't wait.

"I can't believe we can't get in," Carol lamented.

"You can't? I could call Michael Brooks, the producer. Maybe he could get you on the list," Meg offered.

"You'd do that? That would be sensational," Holly enthused.

"I told you Meg was the greatest," Carol said.

At least someone *still thinks I'm a good friend,* she thought, enjoying herself.

The next day, Meg was surprised to find Roxanne at the door to the Pryor summer house. She held a small garment bag up by way of introduction. "I hope I'm not bothering you. I just don't want my dress for the hop to wrinkle. With the humidity," she said stiffly. "So if I could leave it here for a few hours . . ."

Meg didn't care how proud Roxanne was being, she was glad to see her friend. "Of course you're not bothering me. You want to come in?"

"No thanks," Roxanne said quickly.

"Where's Theresa?" Meg asked.

"She's got a boyfriend down here," Roxanne answered. "Well, I better go."

Meg stopped her before she could walk off. "You know, if you want to, you could get ready here. Since your dress is . . . here."

"No, that's all right. I was just looking for a place—"

"To keep your dress, I know. Roxanne, why don't you just stay here? My mom made strawberry slushes." Roxanne *loved* strawberry slushes. "We're having a crab feast. I'm not saying we have to hang out, but at least you'll have a place to stay after the hop. Besides, you drove all the way down with Theresa—isn't that torture enough?"

Roxanne agreed only to spend the afternoon at the boardwalk with Meg, just like old times. The Thorns were performing live, and the girls wove their way through the throngs of people gathered. Reaching the saltwater taffy booth, they ordered their usual. "Half a pound of taffy, please," Roxanne requested.

"Same for me. All strawberry," Meg said.

"Except for two bananas—," Roxanne put in.

"And a peppermint," the girls finished in unison. The taffy woman stared at them as though they were crazy.

"The peppermint's refreshing, for after," Roxanne explained.

"Meg!" the girls heard. They turned to see Carol and Holly waving and making their way down the boardwalk.

"Well, look who found her way over from the Crest," Roxanne commented quietly.

"Meg, you should come back to the Crest this afternoon," Carol said eagerly.

Meg cringed. She could only imagine what Roxanne was thinking.

"And we'll see you tonight at the hop, right?" Carol asked.

"Um, yeah," Meg said, wishing she'd thought to mention to Roxanne before now that they were coming.

"Thanks for getting us in, Meg," Holly said. "So sweet of you."

Carol and Holly headed off and Roxanne whirled to face Meg, eyes blazing. Whatever headway Meg had made in repairing their friendship, she knew, was now gone.

"How fun! The Crest yesterday and tonight Carol gets to be your guest at the hop!" Roxanne said sarcastically.

"I thought I was going alone," Meg protested weakly.

"This should really seal you in with the Crest crowd," Roxanne snapped.

* * *

Despite her feelings about Carol and Holly, Roxanne agreed to go to the hop with them all. But it wasn't long before Meg began to wish that she *hadn't*. The hop was humming with energy.

"So is this what it feels like to be on the show?" Carol asked, dancing her heart out to the Kinks.

"Pretty much," Meg answered.

"It's exactly the same," Roxanne answered. "Only on the show, there are cameras, and Dick Clark, and all the dancers actually *know* how to dance." She shimmied a little, breaking out her trickier moves to prove her point. Carol glared at Roxanne and shimmied right back. Suddenly the two were locked in a dance competition.

Steve sidled up to Meg, rolling his eyes. "I take it those two are getting along," he commented wryly.

"Like cats and dogs," Meg agreed.

As the song came to a finish, Meg realized that Roxanne and Carol were nowhere to be found. "I wonder where Carol went?" she asked Steve.

"Maybe she and Roxanne are competing to see who can get to the ladies' room first," he joked.

Behind the podium, Michael thanked the Kinks and introduced the DJ. "While the Kinks take a break, let me thank Ron Diamond for coming down here. Why don't you show these people what you do best?" he said. DJ Ron cued up "Under the Boardwalk" by the Drifters, and couples began to move together on the dance floor.

"You wanna dance?" Steve asked, surprising Meg.

She looked around nervously for Carol, not wanting to do anything to offend her.

"Don't worry, Carol won't mind," Steve said, reading her thoughts. He took her by the hands and they began to dance.

Their closeness made Meg uncomfortable. "Carol's great . . . really nice," she said.

"Yeah, she is," Steve agreed. But his eyes were boring holes through Meg. "You know, I've always wanted to dance with a TV star. You're a good dancer," he said, pulling her a little bit closer.

"My boyfriend, Luke, he's a good dancer, too," Meg said abruptly. She was getting strange signals from Steve. Signals she wasn't interested in reading.

After the hop, Meg and Roxanne walked down the Wildwood pier. Roxanne looked unhappy. "I know you don't want to hear this," she said, "but Carol was telling Holly horrible things about you. I overheard her."

Meg was shocked. "Roxanne—that's ridiculous. Why would she do that?"

"I don't know. She didn't know I heard, but I did," Roxanne admitted, sounding miserable. "She's not your friend, Meg."

"Roxanne, can't you stop? This has been going on for weeks now," Meg said, thoroughly exasperated.

"Meg, you have to listen to me," Roxanne pleaded.

"No, Roxanne. Not this time," Meg said with finality.

"She only likes you because of *Bandstand*. She got you to break in for her picture and to invite her to the hop. You don't see it because you want to be one of them. But you're not, Meg."

Roxanne's words struck a chord of truth, but Meg pushed the thought away. "You're wrong," she said.

"I meant that as a good thing. I wouldn't want you to be one of them. They're horrible," Roxanne said, urgency rising in her voice.

"Carol's not horrible. She liked you, Roxanne, even though her friends said you were pushy and loud. And I defended you," Meg said. "Now I wish I hadn't." Meg knew what she said had hurt Roxanne terribly, but she couldn't help it.

The tears Roxanne had been holding at bay

finally spilled over. She opened her mouth to reply, but then thought better of it.

Instead, she turned and walked away.

Shaking, Meg made her way back toward the hop, looking for Carol to find out if what Roxanne had said was true.

She didn't have to look for long. Carol and Holly were standing beneath the pier talking. "Hi," Meg said, approaching them. "I was just . . . Carol, I know this sounds crazy, but I just . . . I wanted to make sure there wasn't something going on."

"Something going on?" Carol parroted, in a mock-saccharine tone. "Like, between you and Stephen? That kind of going on?"

"What are you talking about?" Meg asked, bewildered. Had Roxanne been right all along?

"I invite you in, take you places someone like you would *never* go, and you pay me back by stealing my boyfriend? You think you're so special because you dance on TV. You're nothing but a pathetic little climber who doesn't belong."

Meg raced home, desperate to find Roxanne. But when she got there, the only person she found was

Patty. "Patty, where is everyone?" she asked, upset and flustered. "Do you know where Roxanne is?"

"She went back home," Patty said.

Meg wandered around to the back of the house, to a quiet stretch of the pier. She was surprised to find her mother standing there, gazing out at the ocean. "Are you okay?" she asked softly.

Helen nodded. "Roxanne seemed pretty upset," she commented.

Meg looked away. There was nothing she could do about it. She told her mother the whole sordid story. "You know what the worst part is? She was right. Not just about Carol and her friends. About me. I really wanted to be part of that group. But when they didn't like Roxanne, I should've stood up for her, more than I did." Thinking back on it, she was ashamed of what a bad friend she had been.

"Sometimes it's hard and we make choices that don't turn out well. All you can do is apologize," her mother told her.

"What if that's not enough?" Meg asked. She didn't think it would be. She owed Roxanne so much more. She couldn't believe she had betrayed the one friend who had always stood by her, who had always put her first. The one friend who had always needed her most.

Her mother didn't have an answer. And neither did Meg.

Eighteen

"JJ?" Meg asked, knocking on his bedroom door. "Did you keep your old driver's permit test? I need to study." She walked into his bedroom without waiting for an answer to find JJ struggling to close his footlocker. Clothes, books, and athletic equipment were strewn about his room. It was the general disarray of someone packing for his first year of college. Meg knew JJ would be leaving soon for Lehigh, but she'd been pushing the thought to the back of her mind. Now, watching him fumble with the lock on his trunk, she found his departure all the more real.

"You going for your permit?" he grunted, not looking up.

"Why not? I'm turning sixteen," Meg replied.

"I'm getting out of Philadelphia just in time," JJ teased. "Can you sit on this while I close it?" he said, referring to the trunk.

"No," Meg said. "If you can't pack, you can't go." She smiled and helped him with the lock, and then waited for him to find his old test. As he dug through the closet, she looked around the room with a wistful expression on her face. Tonight would be her big brother's last night at home.

It was barely dawn when the Pryors said good-bye to JJ. It was hard for all of Meg's family. After Jack and JJ loaded up the car, Patty, Will, Meg, and Helen created a reception line of sorts. JJ bent down low to bid farewell to a sniffling Will. "You know what's great about me being gone? You can have the comic books I left in the garage. Even the Fantastic Four ones if you don't ruin them. And you get the room all to yourself," JJ said, tousling Will's hair.

"How long is this gonna take?" Patty whined.

JJ turned to her, taking her by the shoulders. "I've got news for you," he said to her quietly.

"Tell me quickly because it's cold out here," she grumbled.

"You're gonna miss me. You can pretend you won't but you will," he said. Then he took off his letter jacket and wrapped it around her.

JJ moved to his mother. "I'll call you when I get there," he promised.

At last it was Meg's turn. She looked at him and realized that as much as he could be bossy, she really appreciated the way he looked out for her. The way that he cared for her. "I'm gonna miss you most of all, scarecrow," he whispered.

"You don't even like that movie," Meg protested, fighting back tears.

"I know, but you do," JJ said.

He got into the car with his father, and the two drove off.

Meg was in the listening booth at the Vinyl Crocodile looking over JJ's old driving test when Sam knocked on the door. As he walked into the booth, she said, "This test's gonna be pretty hard. What's the speed limit in a school zone?"

"Fifteen miles an hour," Sam said reflexively.

Meg cocked an eyebrow at him. "Okay, maybe not that hard for you."

He smiled. "You're gonna do fine," he assured her.

Meg sighed. "I hope so. This summer's been so, so . . . I don't know. It'd just be nice to get my permit."

Sam nodded with understanding. "You and Roxanne still . . ."

"Uh-huh. I don't think we're ever going to make up. She's not even coming to my Sweet Sixteen party," Meg said glumly. This was perhaps the biggest blow of all. She and Rox had been planning their Sweet Sixteens for as long as she could remember, and now Roxanne wasn't even going to be a part of hers.

"More cake for the rest of us," Sam said, trying to cheer her. Meg appreciated the effort. But it wasn't the same thing as having her friend back.

Coming out of *Bandstand* the next afternoon, Meg was startled by a voice she hadn't heard in quite some time. "Meg? Meg Pryor? I almost didn't recognize you."

"Yes, it's been a while, Mr. Bojarski," Meg replied politely.

"I dunno if Roxanne told you, I got a great new job selling paint in Pittsburg. Just sold a whole school's worth last week," he told her, sounding hopeful. "Spent most of the money on this." He held out a gold charm bracelet. "Could you give it to her when you see her?"

"Mr. Bojarski, we're not really friends anymore," Meg replied.

"Look, I understand maybe she's told you a few things. How I haven't been around much. How I haven't been much of a father," he said, a pleading note creeping into his voice. He seemed sad, tired, and old. Older than Meg's parents, in some way.

"She doesn't really talk that much about you at all," Meg said softly.

His face fell. He held out the bracelet again.

"Meg," he begged. "Just give this to her. Please."

"We did it!" Meg shouted, racing into the Vinyl Crocodile joyfully. She wrapped her arms around Luke and kissed him full on the lips. He gave in for a moment, then pulled back, indicating the gaggle of teenaged customers ogling them.

"You passed?" he surmised.

Sam stepped forward. "We passed the written test."

Meg nudged her boyfriend. "So, when do we start *driving*?" she asked, not so subtly.

"Why are you looking at me?" Luke asked suspiciously.

"Didn't Mr. Greenwood leave you his car?" she asked.

"Meg, I value both my job and my life," Luke said warily. But after much prodding, he finally relented and let them both take turns driving, while he sat clutching the armrest with white knuckles.

After what seemed like an eternity, Meg pulled

the car over. "How'd I do? For a first-timer?" she asked eagerly.

Luke clenched his teeth. "Fine," he said, in a strained voice.

Meg prepared to get out of the car and popped the clutch in the process—the car sputtered, then stalled.

"You popped the clutch," Luke said, more in amazement than anything else.

Meg looked at him questioningly. "Is that good?" she asked.

When Meg got home that night she overheard her parents and Uncle Pete discussing the bodies of three civil rights workers who were missing in Mississippi. The police were conducting a search for them, but hadn't turned them up yet. In the meantime, racial tensions were high. In Philly, the mayor had imposed a curfew for the colored people. They were expected to be indoors by nine—for their own protection. Meg had heard all about it. She wasn't sure she understood it, though.

"What do they do, the FBI, when they look for people?" Helen asked.

"Comb the woods for bodies, dredge the swamps, even look up in the trees. They found six bodies, all colored boys, since they started looking," Pete answered.

"What the hell's happenin' to this country, anyway?" Jack mused aloud.

"Jack," Helen admonished, catching sight of Meg.

"It's all right, I know about it," Meg said.

"'Course, you could say those three boys were looking for trouble," Pete continued.

"By registering voters?" Helen asked. Meg knew her mother had been involved in voter registration. "Is there any chance they're still alive? What do you think?"

"Not a clue," Pete said. He checked his watch and rose from the table. "Hey, Jack . . . I didn't want to bring this up in the store, in front of Henry, but maybe it'd be a good idea to put off the opening."

Meg's father had been planning to open up a second branch of his shop down in Sam and Henry's neighborhood. Meg was surprised to hear that her uncle thought that maybe now they shouldn't. She hadn't realized that things had gotten that bad.

"Girard Avenue?" Jack said, sounding as disbelieving as Meg felt.

"I'm just saying, if things heat up, it's gonna be in that part of town," Pete said.

* * *

Later that evening, Meg went over to Roxanne's apartment. "I'm sorry to bother you," she said. "I know we're not talking. I know we're not friends. But I'm supposed to give you this."

Roxanne looked at the charm bracelet Meg held out. It was nice, no question about it. "Supposed to? Who's it from?" she asked.

"Your dad. He asked me to give it to you," Meg explained. "It's nice," she said.

Roxanne handed the bracelet back to Meg. "Give it back to him," she said. "Or keep it yourself. I don't really care."

With that, she closed the door, leaving Meg standing on her doorstep.

The next day at *Bandstand*, Roxanne squeezed her way next to Meg on the bleachers. "What did my father say? When you gave him back the bracelet?" she asked.

Meg looked at her for a moment. "I thought we weren't talking," she said.

"We're not," Roxanne agreed. She was silent briefly, but the suspense was killing her. "Did he say he's going back to Pittsburg?"

"I didn't see him yet. But if you want to know what I think—"

"I don't," Roxanne said quickly.

"Of course you don't. Because you don't think people deserve a second chance. So you just give up. Well, he's your dad, Roxanne. And maybe he hasn't been a very good one, but at least he's trying now. So, here"—she pressed the bracelet into Roxanne's hand—"give it back to him yourself." She stood up and headed off to another section of the bleachers.

Meg's encounter with Roxanne had left her feeling grouchy for her driving lesson with Luke and Sam. She wasn't the only one. On the news it had been announced that they'd found the three workers in Mississippi— dead. Emotions were running high all over.

Again, Meg found herself in the driver's seat with Sam waiting patiently in the back. Luke, however, stood outside of the car, keys in hand. "You're not getting the keys until we go over shifting again," he said testily.

"We've been over it five hundred times. Sam, haven't we been over it five hundred times?" she complained.

"Let's just do this," Sam snapped.

"What's the hurry, Sam? We've got plenty of time," Luke said.

"No. Some of us have to be home by curfew," Sam said sullenly.

Meg and Luke were quiet for a minute, not knowing what to say. "I know," Meg said, finally. "That curfew isn't fair."

"No, it isn't," Sam said.

"My uncle Pete says it's the mayor who—"

"Your uncle's a cop. Of course he blames the mayor," Sam argued.

"I *said* I thought the curfew was wrong. Besides, what's the difference if my uncle's a policeman?" Meg asked, getting irritated. She knew that life in Philly was difficult for Sam, but she didn't understand why he seemed angry at *her*. "If you think—"

"You gonna start thinking for me again? Telling me how you know what I'm feeing?" Sam said, flaring up.

"Sam, you don't have to get angry," Luke started, trying to diffuse the tension.

"I was just . . . we're both upset Sam. I'm upset *for* you, and if that's telling you what you're feeling—"

"Never mind. Just, never mind," Sam interrupted.

"Why do you have to act like we're on different sides?" Meg shouted, frustrated.

"Because we are!" Sam yelled. He got out of the car, slammed the door behind him, and stalked off.

* * *

That evening, Meg answered the door and found Roxanne standing on the front steps.

"So I just need to know. Should I wear my blue dress? The one with the pleats? Or the really elegant one from prom?" Roxanne asked.

"I don't understand," Meg said.

"To your Sweet Sixteen."

Meg beamed, wrapping her arms around Roxanne. "I don't think you should wear either of those. You're gonna need a grass skirt," she told her.

"You're doing a Hawaiian theme? That's so cool," Roxanne said, doing a little hula dance.

Meg couldn't help but notice the gold charm bracelet dangling from Roxanne's wrist. She grabbed at Rox's hand gently. "What happened with your father?"

"Nothing. Not yet. I'm still not sure if he deserves a second chance," Roxanne said.

"Thank you for letting me have one. I'm really sorry for what I did," Meg said. "You hungry?" she asked.

Roxanne grinned. "Starving," she said, as she made her way to her place at the dining-room table.

Nineteen

"**I** was just saying that maybe Mom shouldn't serve the sherbet in coconut shells because that's not really authentic," Patty said.

"You can be authentic for *your* Sweet Sixteen. If you live that long," Meg retorted.

Meg, Patty, and Will were helping Helen prepare for Meg's birthday party. They were all a little on edge. JJ had been cut from Lehigh's football team and they were waiting for Jack to bring him home. His leg had never healed properly and now he wouldn't be able to play football ever again. Meg felt terrible for him.

"How come JJ went to Uncle Pete's?" Will asked, giving voice to the question they all had.

"Probably because he got kicked off the football team, Will. And was probably embarrassed. I'd be embarrassed," Patty explained, turning to Meg. "Wouldn't you?"

Meg felt a fresh rush of sympathy for her brother, knowing how distraught he must feel. "I don't know what I'd be," she answered. She crossed over to the kitchen table, where her mother was assembling black licorice into spiral disks resembling 45s, each adorned with a label that said, "Meg's Sweet Sixteen."

"Sally, Luke, Roxanne, Andrea," Meg checked off out loud. "Sam."

"I thought Sam wasn't coming," Helen said.

"He's not," Meg said quietly. She paused, then continued to go through the favors. He had called her earlier to say that he didn't want to be friends anymore. He thought they were too different, but Meg wasn't willing to believe him.

The next evening, the finishing touches were being put on the luau. But then JJ came home, and chaos ensued.

He had enlisted.

The Marines.

Jack thought it was a good idea, a practical decision. JJ was eighteen and had the right to choose his own course. This way, the Marines would pay for college and he could still train to be an astronaut as he had always wanted. Helen was devastated at the prospect of JJ serving, and angry that Jack had allowed their son to make this decision without consulting her.

Meg was mainly worried. She wasn't sure what was going on over in Vietnam, but she didn't want JJ in the middle of it. Most of all, though, she wanted what was best for him.

She turned Sam's party favor over in her hands. Why did things have to be so complicated?

"Why don't you give that to him?" Helen suggested gently, standing over Meg's shoulder. "Put yourself in his shoes . . . it would be hard for him, being here."

Meg knew her mother was right.

Meg found Sam at the Girard Avenue store, getting it ready for opening day. She rapped on the door and he let her inside. Meg handed him his party favor.

"I know you think we're not friends. That we're too different," she said. She wanted him to understand that she was *trying*, that she wanted to see things from his point of view as much as she could.

"We are, Meg," Sam insisted.

"No. When I was having that bad time with Roxanne this summer, you were the only person I could talk to about it. When you and Anita broke up for those two weeks, who did you ask for advice? And when Luke is so annoying that I just want to kill him, who do I call?"

Sam had to crack a smile. "Only 'cause no one else wants to hear about it," he said.

She smiled too. "We *are* friends, Sam. And if you don't want to come to my party tonight, that's okay. I mean, it's not okay, but I understand. But we are friends, and—"

She stopped when she heard the sound of glass shattering a few blocks away. What was that? She had seen a few people scampering down the street on her way over, and had heard one woman calling for her daughter to get inside. She and Sam looked at each other, then tentatively stepped outside of the store. They couldn't see anything in either direction.

Then another window shattered.

"What do you think that is?" Meg asked.

Sam paused, a grim expression on his face.

From inside the store, the telephone rang. Sam ran for it. Meg could hear his side of the conversation. It didn't sound like good news.

"I'm fine," he said. "Yes, we can do it. . . . Nothing, I'm gonna go board up the windows." He hung up the phone and flicked on a television set. Then he crossed to the front door and locked it. "Gotta move these TVs from the front," he said to Meg. "Your uncle's coming here."

"Maybe I should leave," Meg said uncertainly.

The television newscaster had just used the words "riot situation."

Sam looked at her steadily. "I don't think it's safe for you out there," he said. "I gotta get some boards." He disappeared into the back. Meg peered out the front window, seeing someone dash by. On the television set, she could see footage of mob violence.

Meg and Sam managed to board up the windows and to move most of the TVs into the back room for protection. By the looks of things, they weren't going anywhere anytime soon.

The phone rang again. Sam answered it, listened for a moment, then passed it to Meg.

"Dad, I—," she began, worried that she was in trouble.

"Listen, Meg. Don't move. Keep the door locked," her father said. She realized instantly that he was far too worried for her to be in trouble. "Did Sam board up the windows?"

"Pretty much," she answered. "Dad, I'm sorry."

"Your uncle Pete should be there soon. Henry and I are on the way. Don't move. No matter what. Do not leave that store."

Meg agreed and hung up the phone. In the distance, she could hear police sirens.

Suddenly, Sam's cousin Nathan and his friend Willy knocked at the door. Sam motioned for Meg to hide. She crouched in the back room. But she could still hear their conversation.

"You gotta get out. Now," Willy said, deadly ominous. "Place is gonna burn down, Sam. Whole street is going down. And you don't want to be anywhere near here when it does."

Meg's heart pounded. What if Willy was right? What if her father didn't arrive in time? What then?

"I'm stayin' here," Sam said firmly. "And I'm warning you, Willy—keep away from this store."

"Don't be stupid, cuz. Man says get out, get out. People goin' crazy out there right now," Nathan interjected.

"I'm not leaving," Sam repeated. "Get out. You leave this store alone."

Nathan shook his head. "It's not up to me." He grabbed Sam roughly by the shoulders. "You're coming with us. It's not safe here."

Sam threw Nathan's hands off of him. Nathan responded by pushing Sam to the ground.

Meg ran from her hiding spot. "Don't! Stop!" she shouted, frantic.

"Meg, stay where you are," Sam warned.

"My uncle's coming here. With a bunch of policemen," Meg said.

Willy looked at her with blind contempt. "Cops aren't in charge, girl." He pointed to the television set. He and Nathan turned to leave the store.

"Get out, Sam. And take her with you. Go home . . . go back to the other store," Nathan said. "But just get out."

Meg and Sam scrambled to lock the doors behind Nathan and Willy. They moved the last of the televisions into the back room and stepped back from the window. Part of the glass was still visible— they hadn't had enough pegboard to cover it.

And then a brick flew through the window, shattering it.

Meg and Sam made a decision. Sam grabbed Meg's hand and led her out the back door.

Outside, the streets were eerily silent. It felt to Meg like the calm before the storm. A car parked on the street burned silently, and a few looters walked by with items in their hands—televisions and radios that Meg fleetingly thought might have been taken from her father's store. What had happened to her city? And when? It seemed like only minutes ago she had come to the store to see Sam.

"Where are we going?" Meg asked.

"To my apartment. It's not too far," Sam said. Broken glass crunched beneath their feet like ice as they walked. Noise from the alleys spurred them to quicken their pace, and at the sound of yet more glass breaking, the two broke into a full-fledged run.

They stopped when they heard a gunshot.

They took cover in an alley, huddled together. Sam grabbed Meg's hand as another gunshot echoed.

As smoke poured from open storefronts, Meg and Sam crept slowly from their perch. The riot was in full swing, and it was terrifying. Cops had brought out their billy clubs and were subduing rioters as looters made off with their stashes. A few people threw Molotov cocktails from their windows, and some men were handcuffed against police cars. In the thick of it, Meg could see her uncle Pete. He grabbed at Nathan, locking him in a choke hold. Willy, seeing his friend in trouble, grabbed a pipe and lunged toward Pete. Willy was almost upon Pete when yet another shot rang out.

Willy went down. He'd been shot by Pete's partner.

"Willy!" Sam screamed, anguished. Nathan and Pete glanced across the street, realizing for the first time that Meg and Sam had seen the entire ordeal.

Sam darted across the street and knelt by Willy, tending to him. Meg ran to his side. But before she knew it, Pete grabbed her from behind, dragging her away. "Let's go. Now," he ordered, in a tone she'd never heard before.

She stood reluctantly. "You're leaving him there? Like that?"

"Someone'll help him," Pete said shortly, tugging her toward the police car. Another shot sounded.

"But what about Sam?"

"Sam'll take care of himself," Pete said, physically forcing her to the car. "Get in."

Meg had no choice. As they pulled away, all she could see was smoke and fire. She heard the screams and shouts of the rioters. In the midst of it all were Sam and Nathan, on the ground, tending to Willy's wound. Willy was unconscious, chest bleeding.

Sam, Meg thought desperately, locking eyes with him from the rear window of her uncle's patrol car. Tears streamed down her face. Sam gazed back at her evenly, sadly. She knew he understood the depth of her friendship and concern for him. But she also knew that at heart, he was right—they were from different worlds. All of her good intentions were undone in this moment, when there was nothing she could do to help him. As the police car sped away, Meg knew that right now, for Sam, their friendship simply wouldn't be enough.

The American Dreams "Dreams Come True" Sweepstakes
Official Rules

NO PURCHASE NECESSARY TO ENTER OR WIN.
Void wherever prohibited or restricted by law.

Limit one entry per person for the Sweepstakes period. Not responsible for: late, lost, stolen, damaged, undelivered, mutilated, illegible, or misdirected entries; postage due; or typographical errors in the rules. Entries void if they are in whole or in part illegible, incomplete, or damaged. No facsimiles, mechanical reproductions or forged entries. Sweepstakes starts on May 1, 2004 and all entries must be post-marked January 15, 2005, and received by January 21, 2005 (the "Sweepstakes period").

All entries become the property of Simon & Schuster Inc. and will not be acknowledged or returned.

Simon & Schuster Inc. will choose one (1) winner in a random drawing consisting of all eligible entries received, and will award one (1) Grand Prize to an eligible U.S. or Canadian entrant.

Grand Prize Winners will be eligible for a chance for a walk-on role on the NBC Series "American Dreams" (the "Series"). All details of the walk-on role to be determined by Sponsors, in Sponsors' sole discretion, subject to availability and production exigencies. Winners must be available during the Series' production schedule and on the dates selected by Sponsors. Grand Prize includes round-trip coach air transportation for 4 (at least one person must be 18 years or older) from a major airport nearest the winner's residence to Los Angeles, CA, hotel accommodations in Los Angeles (2 standard rooms, double occupancy) for 3 days and 2 nights, ground transportation to and from the airport to the hotel, and a visit to the NBC set of the television series "*American Dreams*," provided that the show is in production during winner's trip. Prize does not include transfers, gratuities, upgrades, personal incidentals, meals or any other any expenses not specified or listed herein. Total retail value of Grand Prize: approximately $4,000. All travel subject to availability. Restrictions and black-out dates may apply. Sponsors reserve the right to substitute a similar prize of equal or greater value at their sole discretion. Travel and hotel arrangements to be determined by the Sponsors. The Sponsors in their sole discretion reserve the right to provide ground transportation in lieu of air transportation.

One (1) Grand Prize winner will be selected at random from all eligible entries received in a drawing to be held on or about January 22, 2005. Winner will be allowed to choose 3 people to accompany him/her on the Grand Prize trip, at least one travel companion must be the winner's parent or legal guardian. Any other minor travel companions must also be accompanied by their parent or legal guardian. The Grand Prize winner must be able to travel during the months of February 2005 through April 2005. If the Grand Prize winner is unable to travel on the dates specified by the Sponsors, then prize will be forfeited and awarded to an alternate winner. In the event that the show *American Dreams* is cancelled, postponed or delayed for any reason, or if any prize component is not available for any reason, then Sponsors will only be responsible for awarding the remaining elements of the prize which shall constitute full satisfaction of the Sponsors prize obligation to winner & no substitute or additional compensation will be awarded. Winner will be notified by U.S. mail and by telephone, within 15 days of the random drawing. Any notification/prize that is returned as undeliverable will result in an alternate winner being chosen. Odds of winning depend on the number of eligible entries received. Sweepstakes is open to legal residents of the continental U.S. (excluding Alaska, Hawaii, Puerto Rico, and Guam) and Canada (excluding Quebec) ages 8-16 as of March 1, 2004. Proof of age is required to claim prize. If winner is a minor, then prizes will be awarded in the name of the winner's parent or legal guardian. Void wherever prohibited or restricted by law. All provincial, federal, state, and local laws apply. Employees of Simon & Schuster Inc., National Broadcasting Company, Inc., ("NBC") (collectively, the "Sponsors") and their respective suppliers, parent companies, subsidiaries, affiliates, agencies, and participating retailers, and persons connected with the use, marketing, or conducting of this Sweepstakes are not eligible. Family members living in the same household as any of the individuals referred to in the preceding sentence are not eligible. Prizes are not transferable, may not be redeemed for cash, and may not be substituted except by Sponsors, in which case a prize of equal or greater value will be awarded. If the prize is forfeited or unclaimed, if a prize notification is undeliverable, or in the event of non-compliance with any of these requirements, the prize will be forfeited and the Sponsors will randomly select from remaining eligible entries an alternate winner.

If the potential winner is a Canadian resident, then he/she must correctly answer a skill-based question administered by mail. If the potential winner does not correctly answer the skill-based question, then an alternate winner will be selected from all remaining eligible entries.

All expenses on receipt and use of prizes including provincial, federal, state, and local taxes are the sole responsibility of the of the winner's parent or legal guardian. On winner's behalf, winner's parents or legal guardians will be required to execute and return an Affidavit of Eligibility and a Liability/Publicity Release and all other legal documents that the Sweepstakes Sponsors may require (including a W-9 tax form) within 15 days of attempted notification or an alternate winner may be selected. Each travel companion or travel companion's parent or legal guardian if travel companion is a minor, will be required to execute a liability release form prior to ticketing.

By participating in the Sweepstakes, entrants agree to be bound by these rules and the decisions of the judges and Sponsors, which are final in all matters relating to this Sweepstakes. Failure to comply with these Official Rules may result in disqualification of your entry and prohibition of any further participation in this Sweepstakes. By accepting the prize, the winner's parent or legal guardian grants to Sponsors the right to use his/her name and likeness for any advertising, promotional, trade, or any other purpose without further compensation or permission, except where prohibited by law.

By entering, entrants release Sponsors and their respective divisions, subsidiaries, affiliates, advertising, production, and promotion agencies from any and all liability for any loss, harm, damages, costs, or expenses, including without limitation property damages, personal injury, and/or death, arising out of participation in this Sweepstakes, the acceptance, possession, use, or misuse of any prize, claims based on publicity rights, rights of privacy, intellectual property rights, defamation, or merchandise delivery.

For the name of the prize winner (available after February 5, 2005) send a stamped, self-addressed envelope to Winners' List, Dreams Come True Sweepstakes, Simon & Schuster Children's Marketing Department, 1230 Avenue of the Americas, New York, New York 10020.

Sponsors: Simon & Schuster Children's Publishing, 1230 Avenue of the Americas, New York, NY 10020; and National Broadcasting Company, Inc., 3400 West Olive Avenue #600, Burbank, CA 91505.